REUNION WITH AN ENEMY

"Well, damned if it ain't Longarm!" Sisson exclaimed. "It seems like a year ago that they said somebody'd be coming to haul me back to the States. I didn't even think it might be you."

"Oh, it's me, all right," Longarm assured him. "And soon as I can manage, we'll be starting back to the prison you busted out of, so you better be making up your mind to do some traveling."

As Longarm stepped to the door, Sisson called, "Listen to me, Long! If you think I'm going to give you any rest after we get started back, you sure better think again! Because I ain't got a thing to lose, and I'd damn sure rather die out in the open than dangling at the end of a noose!"

— TABOR EVANS —

LONGARM

AND THE DENVER BUST-OUT

JOVE BOOKS, NEW YORK

LONGARM AND THE DENVER BUST-OUT

A Jove Book / published by arrangement with
the author

PRINTING HISTORY
Jove edition / May 1991

ISBN: 0-515-10570-8

Jove Books are published by The Berkley Publishing Group,
200 Madison Avenue, New York, New York 10016.
The name "JOVE" and the "J" logo
are trademarks belonging to Jove Publications, Inc.

PRINTED IN THE UNITED STATES OF AMERICA

10 9 8 7 6 5 4 3 2 1

LONGARM

AND THE
DENVER BUST-OUT

Chapter 1

Longarm woke with a start. The moment he opened his eyes he was aware that the time-sense which usually worked while he was sleeping had somehow failed to function properly. On most mornings the first thing he saw when he woke up was the soft gray rectangle created by the light of dawn glowing through the shade of the window across the room from his bed.

This morning the window did not show at all, not even in outline at the edges. Longarm frowned when he searched the wall for the usual bright golden glow where the gap between shade and windowpane usually brought a promise of sunrise into his room. Now the wall was dark, lacking even the suggestion of a glimmer.

Longarm decided at once that he had no desire to get up in the pre-sunrise gloom. He closed his eyes and settled back on the pillow, but its feathers seemed to have been replaced by small bricks while he slept.

1

Half-rising, Longarm pushed and poked at the thinly filled pillow, trying to loosen its packed feathers, but the pillow resisted his poking. It stayed firm and unyielding, and when he settled back again he found that the pillow still was not thick enough to support his head properly.

Longarm was not accustomed to waking so early unless he'd locked into his mind the night before that he had to rise earlier than usual. He'd been lying on his back; now he turned on his side, trying to find a more comfortable position, one that would recall sleep. In his new posture his head sagged uncomfortably. He folded the thin pillow to double its bulk under his head, but when he dropped his head back the extra bulk placed his neck in a cramping slant.

For a few moments he lay in his new position without moving, reminding himself silently that there'd been many times during field assignments when he'd slept soundly in much less comfortable beds—and more often than not in no bed at all. But his mental encouragement did nothing to help him resume his broken slumber. None of his efforts had been effective in lessening his discomfort. Tossing the thin blanket aside, he stepped barefoot to the window, where he pulled aside the shade and peered out through the widened crack.

Longarm saw that for Denver it was a typical beginning-of-winter morning. Above the housetops the eastern sky was tinged with a faint hue of pink, but a glance was enough to tell him that the sun would bring no golden rays for another half hour or more. Even in the darkness he could see that the ground was whitened by a thick film of what he first thought was snow. After a moment of inspection in the starshine from the still-dark

2

sky, he could see that instead of snow the white coating was a heavier frost than was usual in the dry Rocky Mountain air at Denver's altitude.

"Any man that tries to fight the weather's a damn fool, old son," Longarm said aloud. "And so's one that tries to sleep when God's told him to wake up. It don't look like you got much choice. You might as well do what you're supposed to, stay up and about and get the day started."

Letting the window shade fall back in place, Longarm reached for the bottle of Tom Moore that stood on the dresser and downed a swallow of the pungent rye whiskey. He ran his fingers over the top of the dressing stand until he found the little cluster of cigars he'd laid there when emptying his pockets the night before. He groped for the little pile of matches he'd laid beside the cigars, and lighted the cigar that he'd clamped between his teeth. Before the match guttered out, he raised the shade of the lamp on the table and got ready to dress for the day.

By the time his cigar had been half-consumed, Longarm had put on his shirt and trousers and reached the point of stomping into his calf-high city boots. After strapping on his pistol belt, he shrugged into his thigh-length black coat; winter or summer, the climate of mile-high Denver made a coat an indispensable garment.

Conscious of the increasingly urgent signals his empty stomach was sending him, Longarm picked up his necessaries from the top of the bureau and dropped them into his pockets: loose change and the little pocket purse that held his scanty supply of gold coins. He pulled a fresh folded bandanna handkerchief from the nightstand drawer to replace the used one in his hip pocket, then dropped a handful of shells for his Colt into a side pocket of his

3

coat and slid his remaining stock of long thin cigars into the inside breast pocket.

With the necessaries stowed away, Longarm picked up his low-crowned wide-brimmed hat and settled it into place, then closed the door of the room behind him and locked it. With his boot heels thunking on the thin carpet runner of the stairway, he swung the hall door open. Dawn was closer now. The eastern sky had begun to glow pink. Longarm stood on the truncated porch for a moment and flicked his eyes along the street, taking stock of the beginning day.

No lighted windows showed in any of the houses that he could see, but the sky's increasing brightness was reflected in a layer of glistening frost that covered the ground almost as completely as a light snowfall. The miniature front lawn of the rooming house was an unbroken sheen that extended to the street's opposite side; neither footprints nor carriage ruts marred the smooth white surface. Setting his feet down squarely to keep them from slipping on the icy frosted earth, and leaving a thin trail of gray smoke from his cigar to dissipate in the still-dark predawn air, Longarm walked carefully to the cinder sidewalk and started toward the Cherry Creek bridge.

As nearly as he could tell when he crunched across the frost-filmed bridge and strolled toward Colfax Avenue, Longarm was the only person in Denver who was awake and moving through the early morning chill. Ahead of him, the Colorado capitol building was now outlined against the brightening before-sunup sky. In the west the sky was still dark, broken by the fading twinkling of only the brightest stars.

George Masters's barbershop wasn't open yet, though light streamed out above and below the swinging doors

4

of the saloons that flanked it. Longarm was more interested in food than he was in a shave. He went on past
the saloons and the shuttered barbershop and turned
into the little hole-in-the-wall restaurant a few doors
beyond the closed store doors. Twenty minutes later, the
growls of his stomach quieted now by a breakfast of pan-
cakes topped with ham and eggs and washed down with
black coffee, he strolled back to the barbershop. This
time he found the door ajar and the lights on. George Masters was busy rearranging the array of shaving mugs and
bottles of hair tonic in the shelves behind the two barber
chairs the shop boasted.

"Morning, Marshal Long," Masters said. "It's a mite
early, even for you, but I guess you got a busy day and're
looking to get spruced up for it?"

"No, George, I just woke up early and couldn't get
back to sleep," Longarm replied. "But if you're ready
to start work, I'm all set for a shave."

"Set down and be easy, then," the barber told him.
"And I'll have you fixed up in a jiffy."

Carrying with him a faint aroma of bay rum, Longarm
stepped out of the barbershop. The stubble was gone from
his tanned cheeks now and his steerhorn mustache had
been twirled into neat points. Masters had done his work
quickly. The sidewalks and street were still deserted, and
though the sky had brightened in the east with a glow of
the impending sunrise, the rim of the sun itself was not
yet visible.

Longarm stopped for a moment just outside the door
while he fished out a fresh cigar and fumbled for a match.
As he fingered the match into a position where he could
scrape his thumbnail over its head, the small sliver of

5

wood slipped from his fingers. Longarm bent to pick it up just as a rifle barked across the street and a bullet sang above his head.

With an ominous wood-splintering splat the lead thunked into the doorjamb. Almost before the crackle of breaking wood died away in the quiet morning air Longarm had dropped prone on the sidewalk. His gun hand was closing on the butt of his Colt as he went down, and when he straightened himself to stretch out flat, the revolver was already aimed in the general direction from which the rifle shot had come.

A second shot broke the still air as muzzle blast flashed from a narrow black slit that marked the gap between two store buildings across the street. Behind Longarm, the tinkle of breaking glass sounded from the barbershop, but he did not turn to look. His eyes were fixed on the opposite side of the street where the sudden burst of red brightness from the rifle shot had outlined the edges of the two buildings that rose flanking the narrow space between them. There the sniper was concealed.

Though Longarm could not see the rifleman because of the angle at which he was forced to look, he played for a lucky shot. Aiming quickly at an imaginary breast-high spot on the side wall of the building on his left, he triggered his Colt, trying to send its bullet to strike the brick wall at an angle that would send the slug ricocheting off its bricks.

Even as he fired, Longarm knew that the odds were several thousand to one against his gamble that the brick wall might deflect the bullet and send it veering off the wall to hit his unseen assailant. After the first shot, Longarm held his fire, his eyes fixed on the dark gap between the buildings across the street.

6

Again the rifle barked. This time its muzzle flash brightened the gap and outlined its sides. The instant of light and the darkness that followed the shot caused the gap to look even blacker.

Behind Longarm, from inside his barbershop, George Masters called, "What in hell's going on out there, Marshal Long?"

Without turning his head, Longarm replied, "Damned if I know, but some son of a bitch in that little crack between them buildings across the street is trying to pick me off. You stay in your shop where you'll be safe, George. I'm going over there after him."

"Wait till I can get my pistol outa the drawer and I'll cover you while you cross the street," Masters suggested.

"There ain't time for that, George," Longarm replied. "Don't show yourself now, and maybe get killed. It's me that fellow's after."

As he spoke, Longarm was rolling along the board sidewalk in the direction of the opening where the still-unseen rifleman was hiding. As he moved, he muttered to himself, "Looks like whoever it is between them buildings over yonder has done flown the coop. But if that gap over yonder's like a lot of 'em here in town, he ain't going too far nor moving too fast. You still got a chance to catch up with him."

Longarm levered himself erect. His feet started to move the instant they were firmly on the ground. He set his course across the narrow street at a sharp angle, one that would take him out of the shootist's line of sight in about two long steps.

No shot had come from the black slit as Longarm rose. Now he took the two long stretched-out strides that carried him almost all the way to his goal. He'd been

7

a target for the lawless too many times in the past to stretch his luck thin. Experience made his moves almost instinctive. He hit the ground again.

Longarm was still short of the position he'd need to fire directly down the narrow passageway when he dived. He dropped flat on the street's graveled surface just as another shot reverberated in the gap between the buildings and crashed through the window of Masters's barbershop with a tinkle of breaking glass.

An angry yell came from George Masters as the noise of his shop window's breaking glass filled the air, then Masters's revolver cracked in an echo to Longarm's Colt. When no answering fire came from the black void ahead, Longarm rose to a crouch and ran for the opening. His night vision had returned by now, and against a faint glimmer of light at the far end of the narrow slit he could see the form of his fleeing attacker silhouetted.

Gambling that the man ahead would not turn and try again, Longarm held his fire. He ran down the narrow gap between the buildings, but before he could catch up with the man in front of him, the silhouetted figure vanished and the glow from the streetlight rising at one corner of the opening showed unbroken as it trickled into the narrow strip of open space.

His boot soles slipping on the moist uneven bricks underfoot, Longarm started for the end of the passageway. Reaching it, he looked to his right and saw nothing. Then when he turned to look in the opposite direction, he got another glimpse of his unknown assailant. The man was still running, and the range was long for his Colt, but Longarm took careful aim and let off the last round in his pistol's chamber.

When he saw the running man break his stride, Long-

8

arm hoped that his shot had gone true. He started toward the staggering figure. As he ran, he reloaded, thumbing fresh rounds into the Colt's cylinder by feel. Before he'd slipped the last bullet into the weapon, the man ahead turned at a corner and vanished.

Longarm tried to move faster, but running on the uneven brick pavement was chancy even when it was dry underfoot. Now, after the bricks had been moistened by the night's frost, his boot heels kept slipping and he was forced to move ahead at little more than a walk. By the time he'd reached the corner where the fleeing bushwhacker had turned, the man he'd been chasing was nowhere in sight.

Longarm was too old a hand to waste time and energy by chasing vanished shadows. Holstering his Colt, he turned at the corner of the street and went back to the barbershop. Masters was sweeping broken glass off the floor. Above the shelf that ran behind the barber's chair the mirrored wall was now broken by a wide jagged-edged inverted vee.

"You got any ideas about who that fellow trying to get you might've been?" the barber asked. "Because if you do, I'd sure like to catch up with him and take the price of a new mirror outa his hide."

"Well, I'm sorry about your mirror getting busted, and you don't want to catch up with him half as bad as I do," Longarm replied. He was taking out a cigar as he spoke. "I never did get a good look at him, but whoever it was, he was sure out to get me. I'd make a guess that he's been watching me for a little spell, figuring how he could bushwhack me and get away clean."

"Which it looks like he did, even if he didn't put a bullet into you."

9

"Hell's bells, George! I been shot at before," Longarm said after he'd touched a match to his stogie and puffed it into life. "It looks like you got your job pretty well in hand, so I'm going to get along to the office and see what sorta job Billy Vail's got lined up for me today."

Although the day was still early when Longarm reached the Denver federal building and climbed the stairs to the district marshal's office, Longarm discovered that Billy Vail had beaten both him and the little pink-cheeked clerk. The door to the chief marshal's office was open wide and Vail was at his desk, lifting one stack of papers after another from the piles that covered its top. Absorbed in his search, he had not seen Longarm come in.

"Well, now, Billy," Longarm said. "Looks like I got here just in time to help you find whatever it is you're looking for."

"You're just the man to help me too," Vail replied. "But before I tell you why, suppose you tell me what's gotten you up so early."

"I guess it must've been the weather," Longarm answered. "I just woke up and couldn't get back to sleep, so I got up and started down here. I figured to be waiting for a change when you showed up, so you couldn't keep on joshing me about always being the last one to report in."

"But you still didn't beat me here," Vail said with a smile.

"No, but I would've, except for some skulking rat that tried to shoot me when I come outa George Masters's barbershop."

Vail's smile vanished and was replaced by a frown.

10

"You mean there was somebody holed up laying for you?"

"Sure to me that's what it was," Longarm replied. "You go to George's shop yourself, Billy. I reckon you've noticed across the street from it where there's a sorta gap between them two big brick warehouse buildings? A place where they don't quite push up against each other?"

Vail thought for a moment before he nodded and said, "Now that you mention it, I do. I guess I've seen it so many times that I'd forgotten it was there."

"That's the same way I was when I stepped outa George's shop and whoever was holed up there started shooting."

"I don't see you've been bleeding anywhere, so I suppose he missed?"

"Not by enough to make a man easy-minded," Longarm answered. "It's just pure luck, any way you take it. I was trying to light a stogie and dropped my match. He triggered off his shot just when I bent down, or I wouldn't be here telling you about it."

"I can guess the rest," Vail told Longarm. "He started to run when he saw he'd missed you, and you took out after him."

"That's close enough," Longarm agreed. "He begun running the minute he seen he'd missed me. You know how things like that go, Billy. He'd got to the next street over by the time I'd wormed through that little crack between them two buildings. It took me a long time to worm through that little slit and get to the next street over, where it comes out. I never rightly seen him again, but I hit him, I'm sure."

Nodding thoughtfully, the chief marshal went on. "I

know it's not the first time some crook—or even a gang of outlaws—has set out to cut you down, but this fellow must've had a really good reason, coming after you here in Denver, on your own stamping ground."

"Why, it don't seem to me it'd make all that much difference where they made their play, Billy," Longarm said.

"It might," Vail said soberly. "I'd imagine you're a little bit more careful when you're out working a case in a place that's strange to you."

"I don't wander around much of anyplace with my eyes shut," Longarm noted. "Not even here in Denver."

"Denver's grown up to be a pretty good-sized town now," the chief marshal pointed out. "Whoever it is that's out to get you wouldn't stand out like a sore thumb the way they would in some smaller place."

Longarm sat in silence for a moment, a frown forming on his face. Then he said, "Billy, you know me well enough by now to know I ain't one to tuck my tail between my legs and run just because there's somebody around looking for a showdown."

"I know it's not your style," Vail agreed. "But it just happens that when you came in I'd about decided to send you out on the kind of job I generally give to a new man."

"And I can just guess what it is," Longarm replied. "You're figuring to send me someplace to bring back a crook that's got his name on our want list."

"I'll have to answer you both yes and no," Vail said. "You'll be bringing back a prisoner, all right, but there's a little bit more to it than that. You might not find this job so hard to swallow, after I've told you about it."

12

Chapter 2

For a moment following his announcement, the chief marshal sat in silence. Then he went on. "That's the job, all right, but I haven't mentioned yet who the prisoner is. When you hear his name, I think you'll see right off that he's not somebody I'd feel safe about trusting to a new man. And there's a little bit more to it than that."

"Spit all of it out then, Billy. You know you don't have to beat around no bushes with me."

"What'd you say if I told you the man you'll be bringing back here is Kelly Sisson?"

"Sisson?" Longarm thought. "He'd be the same one that likes to call himself Killer Sisson?"

"There's only one outlaw I know of by that name," Vail replied. "And I don't suppose you've forgotten him."

"I got good reason not to, Billy. He's the one I had to chase all the way to the Rio Grande, and I got into what

13

was almost a shooting fuss with the *rurales* because he was wanted in Mexico as bad as he was here. Then I come damn close to having to kill him before I tamed him down enough to bring him back to stand trial."

"Which he did, if you remember," Vail added. "And I imagine you recollect that he got a hanging sentence."

"Sure, I do. But how come he's still alive and how in hell did he get loose, Billy? The way I figure, he ought've dropped down through the hangman's trap a year or more ago."

"By rights, he should have," Vail said. "But he found some jackleg lawyer who claimed he didn't get a fair trial, and the lawyer turned up a judge that gave him a stay of execution. I don't know all the ins and outs about him getting away, but he took off for Canada. I guess he thought he'd change his luck, going north, but when he tried to sneak across the border into Canada the Mounties nabbed him, or so I've heard."

"I guess you got to give credit to the Mounties," Longarm noted. "Next to our own outfit, I'd say they're about the best there is."

"I can't argue with you about that, but the Mounties didn't want to keep him. They didn't come right out flat and say so, but I'm guessing it was because they had to chase him across our side of the border before they finally caught up with him."

"As I recall, they ain't supposed to do that," Longarm said. "Not unless there's been some rules changed in their outfit. It's like you've told us deputies we can't go across the border into Canada."

"That's right," Vail agreed. "I don't even know where they really caught up with Sisson, but I've got a hunch it was on our side of the border. All I'm sure of is that he's in jail in a place in Washington Territory that nobody around here's ever heard of, a little town called Moses."

"Moses," Longarm repeated. "I've moseyed around some up in that part of the country, but I sure never heard of it."

"Whether you have or not, you've got a friend there, a deputy sheriff named Fred Carter."

"Fred Carter!" Longarm exclaimed. "I ain't seen hide nor hair of that rascal for more years than I like to think about, Billy! Why, me and him deputied together before I got on the marshal's force."

"Well, he hasn't forgotten you, Long. And I guess he knows you're still on the force, but he doesn't know where you are, because he sent you a message in care of the Justice Department that he's holding Sisson for you to pick up."

"That sounds like something old Fred'd do," Longarm said. "When he sets out to do a job, he does it right to the tee."

"I've figured that out myself," Vail said. "My guess is that when the Mounties nabbed Sisson they found out he already had a hanging sentence on this side of the border. They figured the best thing to do was get rid of him once and for all, so they just turned him over to the closest place to them that had a jail and told the sheriff to let the Justice Department brass in Washington know where he was."

"And the deputy sheriff just happened to be Fred Carter," Longarm said. "It all makes sense, when you look at it right."

"Of course it does," Vail agreed. "Whoever in the department got Carter's message looked your name up in the files and put it on the night telegraph wire to me. There wasn't any order with it, but there didn't have to be. They knew I'd send you or somebody to go after Sisson and bring him back."

"I guess Fred figured he was doing the right thing," Longarm commented. Then he frowned and went on. "But what I can't figure, Billy, is why nobody passed on the word to you when this Sisson fellow got loose."

"Don't ask me how everything happened, because I don't rightly know all the ins and outs of that part of the case," Vail said.

"But what it boils down to is that we're going to have to bring that damn Sisson back here to be hanged," Longarm stated. "Why don't the big brass in Washington just let Fred Carter take him up the gallows walk where he's at, if only for killing Collins."

"You know what it's like back East at headquarters, Long. They've got some butter-brained ninnies in the department now, pen-pushers who don't have the first idea what the real world's like. They've decided that when an escaped federal prisoner's recaptured, he's supposed to be sent back to where he escaped from instead of the nearest federal pen."

"Oh, I can see where you ain't got much of a way to go," Longarm said when Vail stopped speaking. "And from the way you're talking, I figure you've picked me out to do the job, even if it means sending me all the way out there."

"Yes, and I guess you know why. If I send you after him, I can be certain you'll get him back here. I sure as hell don't want to go through any more red tape than I have to, and my guess is that even if Sisson is as slippery

16

as he's always been, I can depend on you to hang on to him."

"Well, now," Longarm said. "It looks to me pretty much like you've made your mind up, Billy. When do you want me to start?"

"Why, as soon as you can get ready. The quicker you leave the sooner we'll be sure that we've got Sisson in our own jail. I don't guess there's any chance of him getting away again before you get there to take custody of him."

"Just what does 'there' mean, Billy? You said something about a place called Moses, which I never heard about before, and Washington Territory takes in a pretty big slice of country."

"This place they're holding him is over in the east part of Washington, as I recall," Vail replied. "There's a lot of new towns popping up there. But you'll have to wait till you get closer to the Territory to find out exactly where it is, because I couldn't locate it on any of the maps we've got here in the office."

"Oh, I don't look to have any trouble getting there," Longarm said.

"Good. I'll have the clerk fix up your travel papers and expense vouchers, and just in case it's necessary, I'll go downstairs to the lawyers' office and have them fix up a warrant and whatever else you'll need."

"I'll catch the midnight flyer then," Longarm said. "And if there's a poker game tonight, I might as well sit in on it till train time."

"There is," Vail said. "But I'll warn you right now, I woke up feeling lucky this morning, and I'd just as soon win your money as the next man's."

"We'll just settle that when the cards get dealt," Longarm told Vail. "And if it ain't too much trouble, Billy, I'll ask you to bring my papers to the game, since I won't show up here for the rest of the day."

"No trouble," Vail said. "But I'm going to be playing a heavy game tonight. Just be sure you don't get your pockets mixed up and lose your expense money as well as your own."

"We'll just see about that when the time comes, Billy. Now, if you don't have anything for me to do the rest of the day, I'm going out and mosey around town. There's bound to be somebody who knows why that sniper was trying to kill me this morning, and I'd give a pretty to know myself."

Although Longarm had known before setting out that his attempt to dredge out information about the mysterious sniper might well be energy wasted, he did not spare any effort. Starting from the Union Station, he began his search for the morning's still-unidentified sniper. Asking questions as he moved, he worked his way in a zigzag through Denver's tenderloin district, the section of town that residents called the "Lowers."

He covered the area methodically, stopping at every sleazy rooming house, flop joint, and saloon. At each establishment he visited Longarm questioned the proprietors, and in some cases the employees, before moving to the next. He did not miss the bawdy houses, though he found most of the "girls" still asleep, alone in their beds at that hour of the morning.

Longarm made much the same inquiries at each call, whether it was a hole-in-the-wall bottle house or saloon, a shoddy hotel or rooming house. But no matter what type of establishment he was visiting, the answers to his questions were much the same.

There had been strangers seen in all the joints he covered, but from the replies that denizens of the district gave in response to Longarm's questions, their resident and transient patrons were saints wearing halos rather than tough-jawed drifters or regular customers. More to his dissatisfaction and frustration, none of the descriptions he received rang the bell of memory that might have given him a clue.

By mid-afternoon Longarm had covered all the more promising establishments. He'd worked right through his regular lunch hour, so he stopped for a belated meal in a little side-street cafe where he ate frequently.

"I guess that fellow who was asking about you earlier today finally caught up with you?" Sid Grayson asked as he slid a platter of chicken-fried steak and potatoes across the counter to Longarm.

"What fellow was that, Sid?" Longarm asked.

"Why, just an ordinary-looking man. He wasn't much wrinkled, but he wasn't no spring chicken either. He didn't sport no mustache nor whiskers. There wasn't a lot about him you could remember, and when you come right down to cases, about all I can tell you is that he had eyes and a nose and a mouth."

"Then he's somebody you never seen around here before?"

"Not as I recall," the lunchroom owner replied. "He didn't even order a cup of coffee, just asked about you and then turned around and went out."

"Wore city clothes, did he?" Longarm asked.

"Brown suit and a stiff-collared shirt, if my memory serves me. What's he wanted for?"

"So far as I know, he ain't on the want list," Longarm said. "Not yet anyways. It's a sorta personal thing. Do you remember whether he had any scars or such-like?"

"Nope." Sid broke off, then went on. "Come to think of it, I do recall one thing. He had a real wide silver ring set with a big turquoise on his left hand."

"Well, that might turn out to be a lot of help," Longarm said. "Thanks, Sid. I'll keep it in mind."

Longarm wasted no time trying to pick up the trail of a man with a turquoise ring. Instead, he went to his rooming house, cleaned his Winchester and his Colt, and packed his necessary bag and took it to the depot. In anticipation of a narrow seat on the hard plush of a leg-cramping day-coach chair where all that he could expect was a largely sleepless night, he checked his Winchester at the baggage window along with his valise. Then, returning to his rooming house, Longarm stretched out on his bed and dozed fitfully until the time arrived for him to show up at the poker game.

"I know it ain't considered polite to cash out of a friendly game when you're ahead, but I don't want to cut it too fine in getting to the depot in time to catch my train," Longarm announced as he pushed his chair away from the table. He swept the modest heap of chips in front of him across to Vail and stood up. "Billy, I'd be obliged if you'll keep tally for me when you men cash in. Close as I can figure, I'm a mite ahead, but I got enough money to carry me till I get back."

Vail nodded. "Just don't bother to bring Sisson all the way here. Hand him over to the warden of the pen in Cheyenne as you pass through. I imagine they'll be as glad to get him back as you will to be rid of him."

20

"By the time we get to Cheyenne on the way back I'll likely be so tired of that damn Sisson that I'd be of a mind to pay the warden to take him off my hands." Longarm grinned. "You fellows enjoy your game. If I leave now, I won't have to hurry picking up my bag and all."

His feet aching from the day's long search for the mystery man who'd been trying to find him, Longarm treated himself to a ride in a hansom cab to the Union Station. He'd allowed himself plenty of time to spare, and after glancing at the crowd in front of the baggage-room window, decided to let it shrink before claiming his valise and his Winchester. All the benches near the baggage room were crowded. Longarm strolled over to the information desk, to a bench where there was space for him to sit down.

He'd just settled down on the bench when he glanced at the little fenced-in booth which circled the information desk. The uniformed attendant was standing at the railing, talking to a man whose back was turned to Longarm. The attendant gestured toward the baggage room and the man with whom he was talking half turned and raised his hand to point.

Longarm had been observing the pair only casually when the man lifted his arm, but the gesture banished all thoughts of casual interest. His attention was riveted instantly on the man's pointing hand. On its ring finger he saw a wide silver band set with a massive chunk of turquoise. The man dropped his hand and continued his conversation with the booth's attendant.

There was something familiar to Longarm in the manner in which the man moved, and he began cudgeling his mind to come up with names of outlaws he'd encountered in the past. Try as he might, he could not come up with a name that matched the few details he could see of the questioning man at the information booth.

Longarm kept running through his mind the names of outlaws he'd encountered in the past, but he could not dredge up a name to match the man's still-unseen face. Moving leisurely to avoid drawing attention, Longarm stood up. He kept his eyes fixed on the pair at the information booth as he advanced with slow easy steps. He'd covered about half the distance when the man turned and stared at him.

Longarm's gun hand moved as recognition swept into his mind. His Colt was out of its holster while the man at the information enclosure was sweeping aside his coat to reach the revolver in a shoulder harness that the garment had concealed.

Longarm's trigger finger tightened as the hand of his would-be killer closed on the butt of his holstered revolver. The .45-caliber lead slug from the Colt slammed into the stranger's chest. Its fatal impact sent him reeling back against the railing. His gun hand dropped as he crumpled to the floor and lay still.

"Guards!" the information clerk shouted as a babble of cries and shouts rose from the passengers who'd been waiting near the information booth.

They were milling around, some trying to escape from the area, others trying to get closer to the spot where the gunshots had sounded. In his enclosure, the clerk was jumping around, trying to attract the attention of the railroad police. Longarm had kept moving toward the information desk's enclosure while the man who'd tried to cut him down was still crumpling to the floor. The clerk had not been able to open the swinging gate of his enclosure because the body of the dead man lay sprawled against it. Longarm holstered his Colt as he stopped at the railing.

"Don't get all pizzilated now," he told the clerk. "Just wait till one of your guards gets here and let him take charge."

"But—but you killed that man laying there!" the clerk stammered, his eyes bulging as he stared at Longarm.

"If I hadn't shot first, I'd be the one laying on the floor there instead of him," Longarm said calmly. "I like it better this way, standing on my own two feet."

By this time one of the guards had succeeded in pushing through the milling crowd. He recognized Longarm and nodded a greeting. "Marshal Long, I hope I'm right when I say that fellow you shot was some crook you recognized."

"You're right as rain," Longarm answered. "It's been a long time since I run across him last, but his name's George Godell, and I'd guess it's still on a lot of wanted posters up in the northern part of the state."

"I can't say I've ever heard of him before," the guard said. "But if you knew him to be an outlaw, that's good enough for me."

"Oh, I tumbled to him, all right," Longarm assured the guard. "He's one of Bill Coe's gang, or used to be. Up at Trinidad. Bat Masterson and him was always clawing at one another, and when Bat quit being the town marshal up there, Godell and me got crossways. We swapped a few hard words once in a while, but it never did come to a showdown between us. I guess it might've if I'd stayed there, but before we passed any fighting words I'd moved on to a new job."

23

"That's good enough for me then," the guard noted. He hesitated for a moment, then with a gesture to indicate the crowd that had now gathered around them he said, "If you don't mind me asking a favor of you, Marshal Long, I'd sure like for you to sorta keep these folks from crowding up around here until I can get some of our men on the job."

"I'll be glad to oblige you, as long as it don't make me miss my train."

"That'd be the westbound limited you're waiting for?" When Longarm nodded the guard went on. "It won't pull in for another five or six minutes. By that time, I'll have one of our own men here."

"Go ahead and do what you need to then," Longarm said. "And you'll be doing me a favor if you ask one of your men to drop in at the federal building sorta early in the morning and tell Chief Marshal Billy Vail how all this started and finished."

"I'll see to it, for sure," the railroad guard replied.

For the next few minutes, before more uniformed railroad guards came up to relieve him, Longarm kept the curious passengers from swamping the enclosure in their eagerness to get a look at the dead man. Then the long blast from the whistle of the limited sounded and the crowd began to scatter.

When he was finally able to leave his impromptu post, Longarm pushed through the remaining crowd to the baggage room. While he was claiming his Winchester and valise, the limited was pulling to a stop at the depot platform. He wasted no time in getting aboard and making a beeline for the smoker.

Settling down in the nearest vacant seat, Longarm pushed his valise under it and leaned his Winchester

24

between the seat and the window. By the time he'd gotten as comfortable as was possible on the brick-hard seat, the wail of the locomotive whistling its departure was sounding. The train began moving slowly ahead.

"Old son," Longarm told himself as he glanced out the window at the lights of Denver slipping by, "maybe this ain't the busiest day you put in for a long time, but it'll sure do to match. And this seat ain't going to feel no softer, regardless of how long you sit on it, so the best thing you can do is catch a little shut-eye before this seat gets to feeling too hard."

Leaning back against the worn plush of the headrest, he closed his eyes and was asleep before the lights of Denver faded and vanished in the distant darkness.

Chapter 3

Although Longarm had traveled countless thousands of miles on trains while covering cases that had taken him far afield from Denver, quite some time had passed since he'd drawn one that took him as far as his present assignment. Now, after changing to a Union Pacific train at Salt Lake City, he was still getting reacquainted with the constant undercurrent of noise that always seemed to be traveling with him. Each of the small repetitive squeaks or creaks or rattles of the coach Longarm had boarded at the Territorial capital was just different enough from those to which he'd gotten accustomed since leaving Denver to renew his awareness of them.

There was the predominant sound created by the grinding of the coach wheels on freshly laid track and the monotonously regular clicking of the wheels passing over each new rail joint. As an undercurrent to the constantly regular clicking there was a recurring repetition of smaller sounds: half-intelligible voices as passengers chatted with one another, squeaks and creaks from the coaches themselves. Then there was the occasional racheting of a coach seat's back as some uncomfortable passenger readjusted its angle, and the almost inaudible noises that were caused by the constantly changing friction of the car's tongue-and-groove board sides rubbing together.

Once the train had left the oasis of Salt Lake City, the monotony of the arid land had been the same, mile after mile. For three days Longarm had spent most of his time looking out the window at the featureless desert landscape that surrounded the Great Salt Lake for many miles in all directions. During those three days, with his dislike for train travel growing, he'd paid little attention to his fellow travelers. As a result he did not notice the man in the dark blue uniform and brass-decorated wicker cap identifying him as the conductor who stopped beside his seat until the railroader spoke.

"Longarm! You old son of a gun, where've you been keeping yourself lately? How come I haven't run into you since I moved over to the UP? Don't you come up this way anymore?"

Longarm had turned when he heard his name called, and was getting to his feet before the conductor finished his greeting.

"Sam Harris!" he exclaimed. "Where in the world did you come from and why haven't I seen you before now?"

"I'd imagine that's because I got on at that division stop at Salt Lake City about an hour ago and this is the first time I've walked the train."

Longarm shook his head as he said, "Maybe it's

28

because you've taken on so much weight since I saw you the last time that I didn't recognize you at first. Why, you've got fat since you quit being a lawman! Looks like railroading's agreeing with you."

"Well, I've got to admit that I do sorta miss pinning on a badge every day, but the rule book says I've got to wear a pistol while I'm on duty, so I still feel about halfways like I'm still a lawman," Harris said. "But I can't say I'm used to these hard caps we got to wear. I'd feel a lot more at home if I could wear my old Stetson. Outside of that, the hours ain't much better, but I get a few days to myself on the turn-arounds, and the pay sure beats lawing."

"I won't argue that with you," Longarm said. "But I'm still managing to get along on it."

"You're going out on a case, I guess? Where you heading for this time?"

"It ain't what you'd call a case, Sam. I don't have to start out chasing after some killer or outlaw. Billy Vail's sent me to bring back an escaped prisoner that some local lawman grabbed onto up in Washington Territory."

"Don't run down chasing outlaws, Longarm. That's the one thing I don't like about what I'm doing now, not being able to go to new places," Harris said soberly. "I'll tell you the gospel truth. There's lots of times I've thought I'd rather be on a good horse, on the trail of some outlaw, than riding the cushions in a railroad coach, without anything on my mind but the little piddling things this job I'm on now calls for."

"Quit it, then. Go back to what you like."

"I would in a minute, if I didn't have a wife and two young'uns to feed and keep dressed decent and all like that. But I feel a lot better right now. We got a long spell

29

ahead when you and me'll have time to visit. When you come down to rock bottom, all I've got to do on this string is walk the aisles every three or four hours and be ready for the station stops."

"How long do you stay with this haul?"

"All the way to Butte, where we connect to the Burlington Northern. Whereabouts are you heading?"

"Someplace called Moses, up in Washington Territory."

"Moses." Harris frowned. "Why, hell's bells, Longarm! That little jerkwater town's a hundred miles from no place! You'll be going up to the Scablands."

"You know, I've heard about them Scablands more'n once, but I never have had a case that's give me a chance to go into 'em and see 'em up close."

"No, and take it from me, you don't want to. You just multiply the Mohave Desert by ten and add some little bare hills that no man in his right mind would think about climbing, and toss a double handful of rocks ahead of you to make your horse break stride every five minutes, and you've got the Scablands."

"You sure don't talk like you'd be real cheerful if you was going into 'em," Longarm said. "But I won't have time to do no gallivanting. I got to take that escaped prisoner back to the federal pen. I've handled him before, and he's a real slippery customer. Nobody can figure out how he managed to slip outa the pen back in Cheyenne just before he was due to walk the last thirteen steps to a hangman's noose."

"Oh, you'll get him there, all right. But don't go sightseeing through the Scablands. That ain't the kind of place any sensible man would want to be." Harris paused for a moment, then dropped his voice to a half-whisper. "Let's talk about something else, Longarm. I guess you still fancy yourself as a poker player?"

"Well, I wouldn't perzactly run to get to a good game if I heard there was one going on down the road a piece, but I might walk a little bit faster than I would otherwise."

"I figured you'd say something like that." Harris paused. "How'd you like to sit in on one tonight?"

"You mean on the train here?" Longarm frowned. "I thought that a little while back the railroads had all gone together and put a rule in the book to stop poker games on trains."

"Oh, they talked a lot about it, and finally got out some rules that gambling wasn't allowed in passenger cars," Harris explained. "That's why we go into the mail coach and keep the doors locked while we've got a game going on."

"Including you as one of the men sitting in, I take it?"

"You know how I cotton to poker, Longarm," Harris said. "Even at that, though, I might feel different if I was breaking operating rules, like checking up on the brakemen to be sure they've done their jobs. We'd all be in bad shape if they didn't take care of the junction boxes and the couplings and all like that. I don't need to tell you that a friendly poker game ain't quite the same."

"Oh, I'll grant you that," Longarm agreed. "But tell me one thing, Sam. It takes five or six sitting in to make a good game of poker. If you got the whole damn train crew hunkered down at a poker table, who the hell's watching out for the train?"

"Why, the ones that're supposed to be." Harris's voice showed his surprise as he replied to Longarm's question.

"The engineer and fireman. They had to be left out of the games, of course."

"Well, that makes me feel better." Longarm grinned. "But with them not playing, how many of your train crew's left to sit in on your game? And where in hell do you find a place to play where the railroad brass won't catch on?"

"I'm the biggest brass hat on this haul, if you want to call me that. We play in the number two baggage car, it's always half-empty. And the ones that generally sets in don't have to be on the job every minute. Two of the brakies, and the baggage-handler and me. That's four. And then there's that real professional gambler that travels this run a lot who makes it five."

"Well, I guess six would make it a little bit chancier. What're you used to playing, table stakes?"

"Table stakes, and five-card stud or draw. It's just a friendly game, there ain't many heavy pots. But there's no limit except the sky."

"You're making it sound like it's a game a man can enjoy."

"That professional gambler I just mentioned says it is, even if there ain't a lot of money changes hands. She don't like to set in on a game with less'n six hands, but you're the first one I've run into that I figured would be safe to invite in to make it six. But five in the game sure is better than four."

"Now it sounds like you're joshing me!" Longarm exclaimed. "Because if my ears took in rightly what you said, that gambler in your game has got to be a woman."

"Oh, you heard rightly. Her name's Ladonna Murphy, and she plays as smart a hand of poker as I've ever run into. Smarter than most men."

32

"And she sits in with you?"

"Why, sure. It ain't often she'll work a town more than a week or so. And I'll guarantee you this, Longarm, you'll get a chance to play real poker when she's in the game."

Longarm shook his head as he said, "Well, I guess I've heard everything now. You mind telling me how she got into a poker game with you fellows? This ain't something I've run into much before."

"You know how it is," Harris replied. "Four-handed poker's not much, there ain't enough cards out for a man to figure the odds on who's holding what."

"Sure, I've seen that kind of game," Longarm agreed.

"And not all poker players can call a close hand right. Me and the other fellows used to argue a whole lot. Sometimes one of us'd get mad at the others and claim they made the wrong call. Ladonna's got a nice way about her when she settles one of our fusses, and none of us argues with her when she makes a call. And she deals and runs the bank, so we don't have to worry counting chips."

"Well, now," Longarm said. "I've only sat in on three or four poker games with ladies, but doing it didn't seem to hurt me none. And I've heard tell that Calamity Jane and Klondike Kate both run a pretty good game when they was dealing, but I never heard of this Ladonna Murphy."

"That don't surprise me none. When she's working a town, Ladonna's too smart to make any kind of stir that'd start people paying any notice to her. And like I said, she never stays in one place very long."

For a moment Longarm was silent, then he said, "Woman dealer or no woman dealer, a poker game

33

sounds good to me right now. I've looked at all the scenery I want to."

"Then you'll be setting in with us tonight?"

"I imagine you've found out a long time ago that there ain't nothing makes a man as tired as not having something to do on a long train trip. And you know good and well there ain't anything I cotton to as quick as sitting in on a good poker game. You've got yourself a new player."

"I tell you what, then," Harris went on. "We keep both of the vestibule doors in the baggage car locked while we got a game going on. That's in case the fireman or the boss brakeman just happens to come through and catch on to what we're doing. But I'll come back here and get you before we start tonight's game."

Three acetylene lights glaring from its ceiling made the baggage car's interior as light as day when Longarm and Sam Harris entered. At each of its ends luggage and bundles and boxes and crates were piled high, leaving a large cleared area under the center light. Beneath the light a trunk had been placed and covered with a shipping pad to make an improvised table. Small boxes from the car's shipments were pulled up to serve as chairs.

Three men and a woman sat around the table. Two of the seats, a folding chair and an upended nail keg, were vacant. Thanks to Harris having forewarned him, Longarm showed no surprise when he gazed at the scene.

"I'll make you all acquainted," Harris announced as he and Longarm stopped beside the table. "This here's United States Marshal Custis Long, only most folks calls him Longarm. He didn't come here to arrest nobody, even if he is a lawman. He likes a good game as much as we do."

Then, pointing as he spoke, he went on. "Longarm, this is the lady I told you about, Miss Ladonna Murphy. That bushy-faced geezer is Cliff Hill, he's the baggage master. Bruce Brown's next to him, he's a brakeman and most of us just calls him B.B. The other one's Frank Arnett, he's Cliff's helper."

Each of the players nodded at Longarm when their names were called, and he returned the acknowledgment in the same manner. Then Harris gestured to the vacant places. "Take your choice, Longarm. I can do fine on either one of 'em."

Longarm did not hesitate to select the nail keg. Out of long habit he chose the seat that would give his gun hand quickest access to his holster. As he settled into place he said, "Glad to get acquainted with you men. And you too, Miss Murphy."

"I'm glad to meet a lawman who doesn't seem to have a grudge against professional gamblers," she replied. "Especially when she happens to be a woman."

"Like I was telling Sam when he remarked about you sitting in on this game here, I've only sit in on three or four poker games with lady gamblers before now," Longarm replied. "But they were real good players, and the games got along as good as any others I've held cards in."

As Longarm spoke he was taking stock of Ladonna. Though she was seated, he guessed that she was nearly as tall as he was, for their eyes met at almost the same level. Her trimly tailored dark gray traveling suit and the ruffles that cascaded from the throat of her blouse to its waistline hid more of her figure than it revealed. Her face was a bit too long and the firmness of her jaw emphasized its length.

35

Neither Ladonna's full lips nor her high-boned cheeks showed signs of rouge, though a tinge of blue shadowing had been brushed on her eyelids to emphasize the golden hue of her amber eyes. Her brow was unusually high, her dark-gold hair pulled back and braided into a bun. She did not move, but kept her eyes fixed on Longarm during the few moments of his scrutiny, examining him in much the same fashion that he was looking at her.

Just as Longarm was abandoning his half-covert, half-open survey Ladonna said, "I hope I pass your inspection, Marshal Long. But I'll guarantee that I'm not wanted anywhere for any kind of crime."

"Well, now," Longarm replied quickly, "I'm sorry if I looked like I was worrying about a thing like that, but a man in my business gets in the habit of looking people over."

"And a woman in my business has to do the same thing," she replied. Her voice was quite level and totally expressionless. "But now that we're all acquainted, suppose we buy in and start playing cards. I'm sure Sam's told you this is just a friendly game. Reds are a quarter, whites a half-dollar, blues a dollar. How do you want them split?"

"I'm aiming to bet from my winnings after the first two or three hands," Longarm replied. While he was talking he laid a gold eagle and a half eagle on the table. "So I'll just buy in small. Count me out ten reds, five whites, and ten blues."

Almost before Longarm had finished speaking, Ladonna was shoving the chips he'd named across the blanket to him. Next to him Sam Harris was settling into place, and Ladonna pushed chips to him without asking any questions. She picked up the deck of cards that lay in front of her and glanced around at the players.

"Draw for first call," she said. "High man names the game, and after that it's winner's choice."

While she was speaking a deck of cards had appeared in her hands as if by magic. Longarm needed no further proof that Ladonna was skilled at her trade, for even his sharp eyes had not noticed her hands moving. She spread the deck with the cards faceup, gave everyone at the table a chance to glance at them, then swept them to her and shuffled the deck three times before spreading the cards once more, this time facedown.

There was a moment of silence as the players slid cards from the spread deck and turned them faceup on the table in front of them. Longarm glanced at his own draw, the queen of clubs. Arnett had received the club king, Hill the four of hearts, Brown the seven of clubs, Harris the jack of spades, and Ladonna the four of diamonds.

Almost before the players had looked at the last card, Ladonna was saying, "Frank's king lets him name the game. What's it going to be, Frank?"

"Why, you oughta know how I feel about poker by now," Arnett replied. "It ain't that I got any objections to stud, but there's a sorta naked feeling I get when my cards are laying out there faceup for everybody to look at. Just plain old five-card draw, Ladonna, jacks or better for openers, no round-the-corner straights or blazes or tigers."

While Arnett spoke, Ladonna was gathering and shuffling the cards. Her deal was swift and accurate, her fingers moving with blurring speed as she dropped cards in neat stacks in front of each player. Longarm picked up his cards, fanning them to expose their values as he brought them up for inspection.

37

His expression did not change as he glanced at the cards and saw the half-profiled faces of three queens: hearts, diamonds, and clubs. The two remaining cards were useless, an eight of clubs and a four of diamonds.

Around the table, the other players were inspecting the cards they'd received. One by one they raised their eyes from the pasteboards and looked at Ladonna.

"Openers?" she asked, swiveling her head as she looked at the faces of the players in turn.

"Oh, I'll get things started, even if my hand ain't what it might be," Arnett said. "But I'll go easy on you. What I got ain't worth it, but I'll open for two bits."

He tossed a red chip into the center of the table. One by one the others followed, adding their chips to Arnett's opening bet. Ladonna picked up the deck and riffled it with her thumbnail as she turned her eyes toward Arnett.

"How many?" she asked.

"I'll just save my openers," he replied as he pulled cards from his fanned hand. "Three'll do me fine."

Now the draw passed to Longarm. He dropped the two useless cards atop those Arnett had discarded. When he picked up the two fresh ones that Ladonna had dealt him he kept his face motionless when he saw that one was the fourth queen and the second the club ace.

Now Longarm returned his attention to following the draw around the table. Harris took two new cards, Hill requested only one, Brown received two, and Ladonna announced that she was taking one card. She looked questioningly at Arnett after she'd laid the shrunken deck aside.

"Well, I helped my openers a little bit," he said. "It'll cost you five to stay in."

Ladonna looked questioningly at Longarm.

38

"Well, now," he said. "It looks like I'm in real fat company. I'll raise the pot a bit, and anybody that wants to go along's going to have to match me. How does five dollars more sound to you?"

Chapter 4

For a moment the players were silent, looking at Harris. He was studying his cards, frowning thoughtfully. Suddenly his frown vanished. He shrugged and said, "It sounds a mite expensive, but my daddy always said that if you don't play you can't win. I'll stay, but I won't boost the pot anymore."

"I sure ain't going to raise either," Hill announced. He was already pushing chips across the improvised table. "Maybe I oughta fold too, but I don't aim to let anybody scare me out. I'm staying."

"I'm in with you," Brown was quick to say. He added his wager to the pile in the table's center as he went on. "And let's raise it a couple a dollars."

"You certainly don't expect me to stay out of the first pot," Ladonna told them. She dropped chips on the table, then turned to Arnett and asked, "How about you, Frank?"

Arnett shook his head when Ladonna looked at him and raised her eyebrows in an unspoken question. As he laid his cards facedown on the table, he said, "This ain't the pot I oughta be in, not with the hand I'm holding. I'm folding."

"I'm not," Longarm said as the other players turned their attention to him. "And I'll even boost it a bit more."

Before he'd finished speaking, Longarm had picked up his necessary chips from the heap that lay beside his cards and pushed the chips into the scatter that had now accumulated in the table's center. He'd allowed his cigar to go out while watching the pot grow, and he flicked his thumbnail across a fresh match to relight the stogie.

"I don't figure Marshal Long for a bluffer," Harris said. He followed Arnett's example, telescoping his cards together and dropping them facedown, as Arnett had done. "So I'm just going to keep Frank company."

"I'm out too," said Hill.

"You know, it sorta looks like this is going to be a two-man bluff-out, then," Brown observed. "But my cards are good enough to push me. I'll just boost the marshal's bet two dollars and see if that spooks out anyone else."

"I think folding's the wise thing for me to do too," Ladonna said. "We'll let Marshal Long and Bruce fight it out. Marshal Long, the bet's passed to you."

"Well, now." Longarm frowned. "I ain't much of a plunger, but it rubs me the wrong way to let a good hand die. I'll cover the raise and boost the pot a little more." He shoved the remainder of his chips into the pot.

"I'm in pretty deep," Brown protested, then added quickly, "But it don't mean I'm pulling in my horns. I'm calling." He pushed all but three of his chips into the pot and looked questioningly at Longarm.

Longarm's voice was mild. "Let's lay 'em down and look."

He and Brown spread their cards faceup at almost the same time. Longarm glanced quickly at Brown's hand. It was a straight from the seven to the jack, but only two of the cards were of the same suit.

At the same time, Brown was staring at the winning hand that Longarm had exposed. Shrugging, he said, "I hope that's the last bad call I'll make tonight, but likely it's not. The pot's yours, Marshal Long. I guess it wasn't my time to win. But the evening's just getting started, and I'll be looking for my luck to change before it's over."

Luck rather than skill or experience seemed to play a major part in the play of both winners and losers as the poker game went on into the midnight hours. Longarm held only average hands and won no more big pots, but careful betting had allowed him to hold his edge by taking two smaller ones. As the minutes slipped by, Sam Harris began to consult his watch more and more often.

Finally Harris announced, "This has got to be the last hand coming up. We'll be hitting a station stop in about twenty minutes, and all of you know what that means."

"We'll have plenty of time for one more quick round of draw, it'll go faster than stud," Hill insisted. "And we'll still be able to clear things away before that stop's whistled." Without waiting for Harris to agree with him, he went on. "I'm dealing. It'll be draw, any pair for openers, so make up your minds and call your bets fast."

Longarm thought about the other players at the table. Brown had lost more often than he'd won, and was still on the losing side. Arnett was a bit ahead. Harris had swept in a hand or two. Hill had played a conservative game from the beginning, but had swept the board twice, aided by a bit of bluffing. Ladonna had dropped out of several small pots, but had won two or three large ones. With the end of the session looming ahead, Longarm was sure that the winners would be more careful in their play, the losers more reckless as they tried to make up for their losses.

"Everybody anteing?" Hill asked, and as the nods and yesses circled around the table he began dealing.

Longarm joined the other players this time in picking up the pasteboards as Hill flipped them to fall in front of him. When Hill put the remainder of the deck aside, Longarm had been dealt four cards in upward sequence from the three of spades, with the king of diamonds making the fifth. The face card was useless, and he decided to play the long shot of winning the final pot by discarding it and hoping to draw the deuce or seven that would give him at least a marginal chance of winning.

"Has anyone got openers?" Hill asked.

"Barely. But I'll open anyhow." Harris shoved a short stack of cartwheels to the center of the table and added, "Five dollars, since this is our last round."

Without waiting to be urged, the others added their openers to the pot. Then Longarm saw the odds against him mounting when Hill began dealing the draw cards. Both Brown and Ladonna drew only one card, as did Arnett. Harris asked for two. Longarm called for the single card needed to give him a straight, and Hill announced that he was drawing two. After he'd made his discard and picked up the card that replaced it, Hill glanced around the table.

"Your bet," he told Harris.

44

"Sure. Let's start easy with ten dollars."

"Not with my hand," Ladonna said, sliding her fanned cards into a single stack and dropping them to the table.

His years of skill at the poker table had taught Longarm the virtue of moderation. He did not raise, but shoved into the pot the amount necessary to keep in the game. From the way the hand had started he saw that it was likely to resemble other last-round hands he'd played in the past. The pot would spurt substantially as the competition narrowed.

Longarm was not disappointed as the number of players dropped to three: Longarm, Brown, and Harris. However, the pot had grown substantially before Harris finally shoved his last chips into the pot and suggested, "Look here, we're all real close to being busted. Ain't it time for us to have a showdown?"

Longarm was the first to agree. He said, "Well, I ain't one to be pushy, or I'd've said that myself."

"Suits me," Brown agreed. He was the first to spread his cards faceup. Three of them were fives, the others were the nine and jack of clubs. "It might not be much, but in a game like this it looked good enough for me to stay in for the showdown."

"It beats mine," Harris said as he tossed his cards on the table. They were also faceup, as Harris's had been.

"I sure hate to look greedy," Longarm told them. "But I got a mixture here that's the real winning hand."

One by one he placed his cards faceup in a neat fan. They were the three of clubs, the four of spades, the five of hearts, the six of clubs and the seven of diamonds.

"I don't guess me or the others grudge you," Brown told him. "You taken the pot fair and square."

"Yes, and it's time for us to get busy," Harris suggested. "Another few minutes and we're going to hear the whistle blowing the next station stop, and we've all got work to do before then."

Ladonna had remained silent until now. Turning to Longarm, she said, "We'll just be in the way here, Marshal Long. And I know I'm ready to call it a day."

"I'd be right proud to walk to the back of the train with you," Longarm said quickly.

They left the baggage coach together, and passed through three chair cars; most of the seats were occupied by passengers, sleeping or trying to sleep. As they entered the vestibule, Ladonna turned to Longarm and said, "I'm in this first Pullman car, Longarm. Not in a berth, though. I was lucky enough to get one of the little cubbyholes they call staterooms that are at each end of the coach. And I don't feel at all sleepy. If you're not too tired, wouldn't you like to join me?"

Ladonna was not the first woman who had asked Longarm the same question, but she'd paid him no special attention during the poker game. There had been some invitations from women whose motive was profit, and he framed his reply to be as frank as her invitation.

"Why, that'd be real nice, Ladonna, if you're sure you ain't too tired yourself. And if you don't want—"

"Too much money?" Ladonna broke in, wrongly anticipating his question. "I'm a gambler, not a whore, Longarm. I've never taken money from a man anywhere except across a gambling table."

"Now, that was the last thing I'd say to you," Longarm told her. "But if what I was starting to say offended you, I'm right sorry. And I got to beg your pardon—"

46

"No," she said. "It was an honest question, and I gave you an honest answer."

"Since we're being honest, I'd best tell you I might be—well, sorta grubby after all the train-traveling I been doing."

"My little cubbyhole of a room has a wash basin," she said as they stepped from the car's vestibule to its interior.

Narrow doors were on each side. Ladonna opened one and Longarm followed her into a small cubicle. It was barely large enough for them to stand side by side between the opened lower berth and a small shelf only wide enough to accommodate the stacks of unopened boxes of playing cards and a few bottles of toiletries that stood on it.

"It's crowded, but private," Ladonna observed. She was fumbling with the hook-eyelets that fastened the neck of her ruffled blouse, and after a moment she leaned toward Longarm and said, "I can't seem to find the fastenings I need. Would you mind?"

Longarm quickly freed the hooks and Ladonna loosened the waist-buttons of her skirt to let it slide to the floor. Her blouse and low-cut slip followed, and Longarm saw that Ladonna's subtly rounded figure was not the result of her carefully tailored dress or the support of corsetry. Her bared breasts jutted firmly proud, their pink rosettes already budding to extend pink pebbled tips. She now wore nothing but a pair of thin silken knee-length knickers, transparent enough to show the dark blurred vee of her pubic brush.

"Perhaps I'd better help you now," she suggested, stepping up to Longarm.

"Why, that'd sure be right thoughtful," he agreed.

47

Longarm unbuckled his gunbelt and laid it on the narrow shelf where the butt of his holstered Colt would be within easy reach. While he levered out of his boots, Ladonna unbuttoned his shirt and pulled it off his shoulders. Longarm helped her as best he could by swiveling his shoulders while unfastening the first buttons of his longjohns.

Even before he'd shrugged his chest and arms out of the undergarment Ladonna had begun working at his trousers fly. Longarm did not interfere with her, but bent to trail kisses along her smooth shoulders. He carried his caresses to her breasts, and as his tongue rasped over their budded tips Ladonna started to quiver.

Wriggling free, Ladonna dropped to her knees and jerked his longjohns down to free his erection. She began to kiss a trail of moist caresses along his rigid cylinder, but this was not enough to satisfy her. While Longarm was still kicking away his underwear her mouth engulfed his swollen shaft and he felt the soft rasping of her tongue begin to pass over it avidly.

Longarm did not move for several moments while Ladonna's busy tongue and softly pulsing lips caressed him. At last he said, "Maybe we better save something for later on, Ladonna. Right now, what you're treating me to is getting me readier'n ever to pleasure you whenever you feel like it."

Ladonna began to allow her caresses to taper off, and at last she released him. Looking up at Longarm she said, "It's helped me get ready too, Longarm. And right now I'm readier than I've ever been before."

As the last words left her lips, Ladonna turned and fell back on the bed. Longarm needed only to make a half-turn and hold himself poised on his knees above her for a moment while Ladonna opened her thighs. He lowered his hips a bit to allow her to place him.

"Now!" she breathed. "I want to feel you go into me now!"

Longarm's reply to her urging was a long firm thrust that buried him fully. Ladonna gasped, then a small scream of delight burst from her lips as his penetration ended. Her body quivered and she tried to lift her hips in response to Longarm's drive, but his full weight was resting on her now. He pushed himself firmly against her, pinning Ladonna to the bed and holding her almost motionless.

Longarm both sensed and felt Ladonna's signal when she stirred and after a few moments he began to stroke. This time he did not lunge as he had in his first full penetration, but lifted his hips slowly for only a short distance before driving downward again. As he began, Ladonna lay supine for a brief time, passively accepting his rhythm, then she started bringing her hips slowly upward as his thrusts began.

Ladonna lifted her arms now, and cradled Longarm's cheeks between her hands to pull his head down until their lips met. Her tongue darted out and Longarm met it with his own. They held their kiss while he continued his slow measured stroking. When he felt Ladonna begin to quiver again, Longarm thrust to make another full penetration and held himself pressing against her. Only the slow swaying of the train kept them from being totally motionless.

After a moment or two, Ladonna twisted her head to break their kiss, and urgency was in the tone of her voice when she said, "Don't stop now, Longarm! I'm almost—"

Longarm cut off her words by pressing his lips to hers and filling her mouth with his out-thrust tongue. Ladonna accepted the caress for a moment before turning her head away to break their kiss.

"I'm burning up!" she gasped. "I don't want you to stop now! Go faster, if you can!"

"Don't worry. I ain't quitting, Ladonna. It's just that I ain't ready to let go yet."

"Please start again!" she urged. "I can't wait too much longer."

"Then don't you wait. I've stopped long enough. I'll do the waiting now without no trouble."

Longarm resumed his slow measured driving. He felt Ladonna begin to quiver and speeded his tempo. Ladonna's response was immediate. Before Longarm had made a half-dozen strokes, small cries of joy began bursting from her lips. She lifted her hips in broken rhythm now as her climax approached, and Longarm adapted as best he could to the upward heavings of her hips.

Suddenly her responsive rhythm broke as she twisted her hips and locked her legs even more tightly around Longarm's body. Her quivers accelerated into a constant spasmic writhing. Her rocking mounted swiftly as her climax took her, and Longarm pressed himself to her, letting her set her own rhythm.

For several moments, Ladonna bucked her hips as Longarm drove into her with fresh intensity, trying to match his thrusting to her erratic motions. A louder scream than usual burst from her throat and she writhed again and again. Longarm could do no more than hold himself in position until she uttered an even louder cry, a laughing sob of unendurable pleasure.

Ladonna's sob faded to a sigh of contentment as her spasms began rippling more slowly, and Longarm made the final few fierce thrusts needed to bring him to his own completion. His muscular body quivered as he jetted and pressed himself to Ladonna, holding himself to her still-trembling body. Then the waves that had been sweeping over them began to ebb and they both lay limp and motionless.

In their shared frenzies, neither Longarm nor Ladonna had noticed that the train was stopping. Their own activity had banished all awareness of the world outside the small dark room. Jarred back to reality by the jolting of the coach as the long blast from the engine's whistle reached their ears, they parted involuntarily.

Longarm swung himself to the edge of the narrow bed and sat with his feet on the floor. Ladonna propped herself up on one elbow and pulled back an edge of the window shade to peer out. Longarm turned and joined her in gazing out the slit she'd opened, but all they could see was the exaggerated silhouette of the train blotting out a portion of the ground beside the track.

"Do you have any idea where we are now?" Ladonna asked.

"Not a notion. It's bound to be a town of some kind, but I wouldn't even try to guess where or what its name is."

"It doesn't matter anyhow," Ladonna said. "I suppose you're going all the way to Butte?"

"All the way there and a long stretch more," Longarm said. "I got a prisoner to bring back from some little jerkwater place up in Washington Territory."

"What a pity!" Ladonna sighed. "I'm getting off at Butte. It'd be wonderful if you could stay there for a while, in some place that was a little bit more comfortable and less public than a berth in a Pullman coach."

"Oh, I'd like that too, Ladonna. But even if I'm pretty much my own boss once I get away from the Denver office, I feel like I'm duty-bound to wind up the case I was sent on as quick as I can. But I'll likely have to wait a while in Butte till I make my train connection. We can have that much time together."

"That's better than having to say good-bye at a depot somewhere."

Even in the shadowed dimness of the little stateroom, Longarm could see Ladonna's smile. He pulled her to him and sought her lips again. This time their kiss was prolonged, and while they held it with their tongues darting in warmly moist caresses, Ladonna's questing hand crept to Longarm's crotch. Longarm's hand moved to stroke her jutting breasts and finger their jutting rosettes.

"If what I feel isn't deceiving me, you're as ready as I am to start again," Ladonna whispered as they broke their kiss.

"I'm ready if you are," he replied. "And if you're like me, it's always better the next time around."

Chapter 5

As he waited on the open vestibule of the long-outdated Continental Northern passenger coach, Longarm leaned as far as possible from the vestibule steps, trying to see the nature of the country ahead. All that he could make out through the cloud of smoke flowing along the side of the mixed drag of gondola cars, boxcars, and flatcars was that the train was on another of the sinuously curving sections of newly laid track that had made up most of the raw freshly tamped roadbed it had passed over.

Longarm was now the only passenger remaining in the single day coach of the mixed train he'd boarded at Walla Walla. There, a change of trains to the new Continental Northern line which was laying rail across the Scablands to the Canadian border had put him into a decrepit passenger coach that had seen better days in its prime, and the last hundred or more miles of his journey had been uncomfortable at best.

He was depending on the advice of the station agent at Butte, who'd assured him that the train he was now on would get him within a dozen or so miles of his destination, even though the railroad was still in the construction stage. Less than a half hour ago, the conductor had warned him that only one more station stop remained before the passenger coach would be cut off on a siding, to wait until the flatcars had been hauled to rail-end and unloaded.

"Then how much further have I got to go to get to that town called Moses? Because that's where I'm heading for," Longarm had asked. "And I'll need a horse. I reckon there's a place at where I'll be getting off that I can hire one from?"

"Well, there's a store and a stable of sorts there," the railroad man had replied. "I'm sure they can take care of you."

Leaning out to look ahead, Longarm saw no sign of a town or other habitation. Then the tracks ahead straightened out, and through a stand of stunted scrub-pine he could glimpse some sort of structure along the tracks. Just then the locomotive whistle shrilled and the harsh grinding of brake shoes warned him that the stopping-place had been reached.

Longarm stepped back to the vestibule platform to get his gear ready to unload. The train was stopping now, but even before he'd had time to drop his necessary bag to the ground and pick up his rifle or to take stock of his surroundings, the engine's whistle shrilled and the short string of cars began picking up speed again. Longarm let his bag fall, took a firmer grip on the throat of his Winchester's stock, and jumped.

Though his feet skidded in the roadbed's loose gravel,

he kept his balance and stepped away from the tracks just as the last cars rolled past him. Longarm released a short snort of relief at feeling solid ground underfoot after the swaying, bouncing, and grinding train trip from Walla Walla.

Longarm did not start at once toward the shabby little shack that stood a short distance away from the tracks. Though it bore no sign, he told himself that the shanty must be a temporary depot. He left the bag where it had fallen on the roadbed beside him and leaned his Winchester across it before fishing a cigar out of his pocket. He lighted the cigar as he watched the railroad cars disappearing through the narrow cut made to equalize the grade broken by the long graveled ridge.

When the last of the cars had vanished on the downgrade beyond the cut, Longarm picked up his rifle and valise and started for the weather-beaten shanty. It was unpainted, the wall facing the track broken by a door and a single small window. The window had no glass panes, and was closed by an inside shutter. Many of the wide boards forming its walls were cracked and warped, as were a large number of the shingles on its low-slanted roof. Behind it Longarm could see the corner of a barn or shed of some sort. It looked to be in even worse shape than the larger building.

Beyond the shanty, a dozen or so small trees were scattered across an arid expanse of ground that stretched to the horizon. In all directions the earth was a uniform yellowish-brown, dotted by a few pale-leafed bushes, none of them more than hip-high. As he drew closer to the little boxlike ramshackle structure a horse whinnied from somewhere beyond the building.

Small as the structure was, it loomed directly in front

of him at the point Longarm had reached, and he could see no corral. There was no sign of a horse running free in the area that was visible to him. He went inside, and as he closed the door behind him, the rattle of another door closing came from the back of the shack and he saw a short wizen-faced man coming toward him from where he'd heard the door close.

"Howdy, stranger," the man greeted him. "Something I can do for you?"

"You can tell me the way to a place called Moses."

"That'd be Moses Lake you mean, I reckon?"

"All I ever heard it called before was Moses," Longarm answered. "I told the conductor on the train I just got off of that was where I wanted to go, and he said it wasn't far off the railroad line."

"Well, whoever it was told you that sure give you a bum steer. The lake ain't too far past that rise up ahead. There's a little squatter's nest with maybe five or six shacks on it about spitting distance from the shore. I guess you could call it a town, because it's damn near as big as a lot of other towns here in the Scablands, but it's called Moses Lake."

"Now, that's enough to confuse a stranger," Longarm said. "There's got to be another town named Moses somewheres around here. I reckon I might find it if I was to zigzag backward and forward for a few days, but there's got to be an easier way. Where'd you guess I might find the Moses I'm looking for?"

"Come to think of it, there *is* another town called Moses. I heard some of the men on the railroad surveying crews talking about it, but that Moses is a good ways further north."

"Well, now, that sounds real promising," Longarm

said. "You got any ideas that might help me?"

"I ain't all that sure just where it lays," the storekeeper replied. "But seeing as how the railroad line's going in that direction, your best chance of finding it is to follow the survey stakes to it. They won't be getting no rail close to it for two or three years from now."

"But there'd have to be a road a man could take to get to it," Longarm suggested.

"Mister, there ain't much of any kind of roads in the Scablands. I never been too far north in 'em myself, and I ain't been here all that long, but I know that Moses is still a hell of a long ways from here, maybe a three-or four-day ride past where the rail-end is right now."

"I reckon you'd know," Longarm said. "From the looks of your store building, I'd say it's been here quite some time. Just at a guess, this shanty's got to've stood here twenty or thirty years."

"Maybe it has, but I sure ain't been here that long. I come up here because the big brass in the front office said I'd got too damn old to be a railroad brakie any longer. And I'll tell you something else. If there was any other place I could go to and still draw railroad pay, I'd sure as hell be there now."

"I can't say I'd blame you," Longarm agreed. "But there ain't nobody that'd like to be someplace else who can get there just wishing about it. Wanting to be don't help you no more than it does me."

"So it don't, but a man can't help wishing sometimes. Right now, I'd say you're the one that's looking, and it'd seem to me like the best thing you can do is just keep on moving," the storekeeper suggested.

"I've done figured that out," Longarm said. "So if you'll rent me that horse I heard nickering out behind

57

your place here a minute or so ago, and some kind of saddle gear, I'll be on my way."

"Horse ain't for rent. Even if it was, I don't run to keeping saddle gear in stock."

"Then what good's the horse?"

"Oh, I got a bit and bridle for him. I ride him a little ways now and again."

While the two had been bandying words, Longarm had been thinking. Although he was always reluctant to exercise his authority in forcing some innocent citizen to give way to his needs, he decided that there was no way to avoid it in his present situation. He took out his wallet and flipped it open to show the badge pinned in its fold.

"I reckon you know what this is?" he asked.

"Why, sure. It means you're a federal man. U.S. marshal, it says."

"That's right. If I feel like I've got to, I can requisition that horse you got out in back without paying you one single penny of cash."

"Oh, now hold on a minute!" the storekeeper protested. "You don't look to me like the sorta fellow that'd take a poor man's only horse away from him!"

"I wouldn't unless I had to. But from what you just said it appears like that's what I got to do if I'm going to get where I'm headed for." Longarm was silent for a moment, then he went on. "I guess I better tell you, my name's Long, Custis Long."

"I answer to Nelson. Mylo Nelson. But most folks call me Nels, and I answer to it bettern' I do to Mylo."

Longarm nodded. "Now, let me tell you what I'll do. For openers, you better keep in mind that I can requisition that horse of yours if you make me do it. I guess you know that?"

"I wasn't born yesterday, Marshal. I know damn good and well what you're talking about."

"Then you'll know that was you to make me requisition it, I'd give you a U.S. Government voucher for rent money while I'm using the animal. That voucher'd be good at any bank or post office after you got the critter back."

"If I ever did," Nelson snorted.

"It might be a pretty fair time before you got it back, but you'd either get it or get paid for it."

"That don't interest me none. I'd as lief the critter stays where it is now."

"Suppose I was to buy it outright then."

"Paying me how? With government paper? No, thanks."

"Was you to sell me your nag, I'll pay you in cold hard cash. How does that strike you, Mr. Nelson?"

Longarm could almost see dollar signs forming in the storekeeper's head as he frowned while juggling the offer around. At last the storekeeper said, "I take it to mean you're talking about cold hard money, not greenbacks?"

"That'll depend on what you're asking, which likely won't be as much as you'll get after we've done some dickering. Remember, I ain't seen the nag yet. It might be just an old spavined bundle of bones, and again, it might not."

"Oh, it's a right biddable piece of horseflesh. Frisky, but not too much so. Like I told you, I ain't rode it much lately."

"Then make me a price," Longarm suggested. "But just because it's U.S. Government money I'd be spending don't go getting no ideas, because if your price ain't right I'll just fill out a voucher and a requisition. Once

I do that, I got the right to take it all legal and proper. I can ride away without so much as a by-your-leave."

"Now, you wouldn't do a man that way, would you?"

"I might not like to, but I'd sure do it," Longarm assured him. "It's in my line of duty. I need that horse to get me where I'm going."

For a moment Nelson was silent, then he nodded and said, "I reckon you would do it at that. Well, come on. If you're going to buy that horse off of me, you'll likely want a look at it before we get down to cases."

Longarm followed the oldster out the back door. The horse in the little rail-fenced enclosure was a roan dapple gelding. Its mane and tail were tangled and its coat was frowsty from lack of grooming, but the animal was neither as old nor as rawboned as Longarm had feared it might be. He glanced at its hooves, and even without lifting them for a close inspection he could see that they had no splits and that the edges of its shoes glowed with newness.

"A railroad blacksmith put them shoes on him less'n a month ago," the storekeeper said when he saw Longarm's eyes drop to the animal's hooves. "Oh, he'll get you wherever it is you're going and back, Marshal Long."

"I'll tell you what," Longarm said. "You name me a good figure and I'll just buy him from you."

"You talking about cash money? Not some kind of gov'ment paper that I'd have to take to a post office or bank, when there ain't neither one closer'n a two-day ride, and me being without a horse means I'd have to go shank's mare?"

Longarm hesitated for a moment while he considered the question and during that moment of hesitation the solution occurred to him. "I'm talking about a voucher,

Nels," he replied. "And the railroad paymaster will cash it for you the next time the pay car is through."

"Well, now, that hadn't occurred to me, but you're right. And I reckon something like thirty dollars'd be what I'd ask."

Longarm had done enough horse-buying and trading during his younger days as a roamingly restless job-shifting cowhand to know that the first offering-price put on a horse by its owner was always twice as much as the final sale figure. He shook his head slowly.

"I might go half that much," he said. "But that's about all the critter'd be worth."

"He's the only horse around here that's for sale, least-ways the only one I know about."

"Now, that ain't quite right, Nels," Longarm replied. "If the railroad's making grade just up ahead, all I got to do is mosey on up to where their work camp is and get me a horse on a government requisition."

"I guess you could do that, if you was a mind to," Nelson agreed. "But I've took in some gov'mint paper before, and it ain't as easy as you make out to swap it for hard cash."

"Suppose I was to offer you fifteen silver dollars," Longarm suggested. "You and me both know it's a fair price."

For a long moment Nelson did not speak, but looked first at the horse, then at Longarm. At last he said, "See-ing as you're on gov'mint business, I guess I got to give a little bit of ground. Take the horse for fifteen. You'll need saddle gear, so I'll want five dollars extra for that."

"That's a fair deal, and I'll take it," Longarm said. He was reaching for his pouch purse as he spoke. "Now, I'll need a receipt for this, so I'll make one out and you sign it. Then I'll ask you to tell me a little bit about the way I need to go to get where I'm heading for, and I'll be on my way."

"There ain't a hell of a lot to tell you," Nelson said. "Except you're going into the top of the Scablands. From what I gather, folks begun settling further up north in the Territory a spell before they did below here. They got water up thataway, for one thing. But you won't be running into railroads or roads of any sort. It's still Scablands up there, just like it is around here."

In the darkening blue sky a red setting sun hung just above the horizon on Longarm's left side and a bit behind him. Its rays cast his shadow and that of his wearily plodding mount as a long distorted black figure on the sparsely vegetated ground ahead of him and a bit to his right. The shadow had been growing steadily longer as the sunset hour approached, and Longarm was not looking forward with any relish to the prospect of spending another night on the hard rock-studded ground.

Longarm had now been in the saddle through the daylight hours of four full days since he'd bought the horse. He'd followed the stakes driven into the arid soil of the Scablands by the railroad surveyors, because he'd seen no roads, no trails, no signs that humans had ever passed that way before.

Regardless of the direction in which he'd turned his eyes during his journey, Longarm had noticed little in the way of differing scenery. Each mile he covered had seemed just a repetition of other miles that he'd put behind him, and glancing ahead gave no promise that the country which stretched ahead would offer any change.

"You know, old son, this is the damnedest place you ever looked at," Longarm said. He spoke aloud to himself, as much to break the monotony of silence as to assure himself that he could still speak and hear. "And whoever it was named it the Scablands sure as hell knew what they was talking about. If it wasn't for them fellows on the railroad survey crew showing you their maps, you'd be in a lot worse shape than you are now."

After he'd ridden in silence for a few minutes, he went on. "Brown rocks and yellow dirt, yellow rocks and brown dirt, and little clumps of grass that don't look like grass as much as it does hay. If it wasn't for that old fellow you bought this nag from heading you in the right direction and telling you how to look for waterholes and places where you'd be most apt to find 'em, you might not've made it this far."

While he spoke, Longarm was scanning the horizon. What he'd said described the land he was looking at ahead almost as perfectly as though he'd just ridden over it instead of approaching it. Low sandy ridges stretched in ripples across the breadth of the horizon. The soil was not totally barren; it was broken in a few places by pale patches of light green grass. Many of these could have been covered by a man's outspread hand, but where even a few of the original sprouts had flourished the grass covered an area the size of a tabletop.

Here and there, rising abruptly from the earth, great boulders dotted an otherwise featureless landscape. A few of them had cracked at some time in their history, and of these some had split into rough hemispheres or quarters to reveal their pebbled cream-colored interiors. The sky held no clouds, but it was deepening into a darker blue in the east, while in the west the red glow of the descending sun lightened its hue to a paler blue.

"Now, if you was to tote up all the time you been in the saddle," Longarm went on, "it wouldn't be much of a surprise if you wasn't getting close to that place called Moses them fellows told you about. Maybe you'll make it as quick as tomorrow or the next day."

As the light continued to fail, Longarm began looking for a place to stop for the night. Finding water was his hope, but given the nature of the terrain he was now passing over he was reasonably sure that the hope was futile. He was mounting a long upslope now, an area where the ground was broken by dark streaks of crevasses zigzagging across its surface, a warning of danger.

His horse was tiring now, and with daylight steadily dimming Longarm was forced to watch the ground more carefully. He reached the undulating line that marked the crest of the rise and stood up in his stirrups to expand his view of the arid land ahead. As he scanned the horizon, barely visible in the fast-dimming light, a gleam suddenly appeared where there had been no gleam a moment earlier. Even while he watched, a second and then a third gleam appeared.

Longarm's sigh of relief was almost silent, more of a forced exhalation of his breath than a sound formed consciously, but it was a sigh nevertheless. Then he said aloud, in a voice just a hairsbreadth above a whisper, "Looks like your luck's about to turn, old son. If them lights ain't coming from that place you're looking for, I'll give you jick, jack, and game."

Settling down into his saddle, Longarm reined the horse toward the light-gleams and toed it ahead.

Chapter 6

By the time Longarm reached the edge of the little settlement, full darkness had engulfed the land. His weary horse was beginning to plod, even to stumble and break gait now and then. He'd held the animal to a slow walk since getting his first glimpse of the lights ahead. Now the roofs of the town's houses had begun to show as dark rectangles against the stars in the deep blue sky.

In the early night-gloom the lighted windows formed a bright path. Longarm counted those in the two lines bordering the street, then made a quick guess of the number of other gleaming rectangles that were scattered around on the high ground that rose on both sides of the thoroughfare. His exercise in mental arithmetic only confirmed what he'd guessed before starting to count, that the town's population totaled perhaps four or five hundred, and certainly could not be much greater than the larger figure.

Longarm's horse was very tired by now. It was breaking stride more often, and he could feel its sides rising and falling more rapidly. Just ahead of him the yellow gleams were broken by a sudden glow of reddish light coming from a building larger than most of those which were visible in the gloom of early night. Longarm recognized the source of the brighter glare even before the thunks of a blacksmith's sledge on heat-softened metal broke the night's stillness. He reached the building and reined the tiring horse to a halt.

Clanks and thunks of hammer blows began sounding inside before Longarm could dismount. His knees were twinging a bit from saddle-cramp after the long hours he'd spent on the trail, but he was sure he'd reached his destination now, and no longer felt the need to hurry. Swinging out of the saddle and stamping his feet on the hard ground with each step to help bring them back to normal quickly, Longarm walked to the smithy's open door and glanced inside.

A husky man wearing a leather apron was alone in the building. He was beside an anvil that stood close to the forge, wielding a sledge, pounding a length of iron rod to flatten it. Sparks flew from the piece of glowing metal each time his hammer clanked with a blow. The blacksmith looked up and nodded when Longarm moved inside, but went right on with his labor and continued turning the piece of iron held in his tongs until the metal grew dark as it cooled. Now it was broadened at one end, the surface of the flared side flattened smooth. Stepping away from the anvil, but still holding the hammer in one hand, the tongs that supported the metal in the other, the blacksmith finally spoke.

"Howdy, stranger," he said. "I'd've swapped hellos

with you sooner, but I couldn't stop or this rod I'm working would've chilled off."

"Sure," Longarm agreed. "I wasn't looking for you to quit your work to jaw with me. Why I stopped is because I just rode in, and I need to find out if this is the place I'm looking for."

"If you're asking what town you're in, this one is called Moses."

"Maybe I got the right Moses by this time then," Longarm said. "Which makes me feel a mite better. I guess you know there's another town called Moses down south of here? If it wasn't that a railroad man I know was on the train I took outa Salt Lake City, I might've gone a lot of miles outa my way."

"Everybody hereabouts knows about the other Moses now." The blacksmith smiled. "That one in the south just took its name from Moses Lake. I guess sooner or later one of us is going to have to change, but so far nobody seems to want to start talking about it."

"It sure threw me off a bit," Longarm said. "But after I asked around some, I got on the right track."

"Sounds to me like you ain't just passing through. You've got business here, I guess?"

"It's business, all right, but it ain't likely to be the kind you're thinking about," Longarm replied. "My name's Long, Custis Long, deputy U.S. marshal outa the Denver office."

"Right glad to make your acquaintance, Marshal Long," the blacksmith said. "My name's Moore, Ben Moore. I'd stick my hand out to shake with you, but I reckon you see why I don't, with all this stuff I'm holding."

"Let's take the will for the deed," Longarm said, falling back on one of the sayings learned during his West Virginia childhood. "The business that I got here is to get a prisoner that broke outa the federal pen back east in Colorado, and take him back there where he can be hanged all legal and proper."

"Then you'd be the lawman that Fred Carter said was likely to get sent after that Sissons fellow they're holding in jail," Moore said. "You know, it's too bad about Fred, but the doctor says he's going to be all right, except he's going to have to take it easy for a few days."

"You mean Fred's sick?"

"Not sick. Shot. Bushwhacked. Just like the sheriff."

"I hope he wasn't hurt too bad."

Moore shook his head as he said, "Fred wasn't hurt enough even to keep him off his job. He taken a slug in the arm and got a graze along his ribs. But from what Doc Forbes says, he's lucky to've got off as light as he did, and not get killed like poor old Sheriff Collins."

"You're saying Fred's the second lawman that's been shot here lately?" Longarm asked.

"He sure is," the blacksmith replied. "Like I said, the first one was the sheriff hisself, but Fred got off lighter than Sheriff Collins did. Everybody figures it was this Sissons fellow that killed the sheriff, but Fred said the smart thing to do was to send him back east, where, you just said, he's going to be strung up for killing somebody else."

"That's right," Longarm agreed. "He'll be hanged there, for sure."

"Fred said something like that too. Said it was the best thing we could do."

"It is, I'd imagine," Longarm agreed. "But I didn't know about all the rest of what you told me. All I know is that my chief in Denver got a wire from Fred, saying he'd caught up with Kelly Sisson and had him in jail. Then I got sent here to bring Sisson back."

"Well, Fred and all the rest of us will be glad to get rid of him. The way he explained it to me, about there not being any witnesses, makes a lot of sense."

"Hold on now," Longarm said. "You mean to tell me Fred didn't actually see Sisson shoot the sheriff?"

Moore shook his head. "Not Fred, not nobody else. But Fred's the one that told me he seen this Sisson fellow start cutting a shuck into the Scablands right after the sheriff toppled down dead. That's when Fred taken after him and finally caught him."

"Then it wasn't Sisson that shot Fred?" Longarm asked.

"Sisson had been locked up three or four days by then. Fred got shot when he was coming out of the jail. That's where the sheriff's office is too. But Fred said it was too dark for him to see who it was that winged him."

"And Fred couldn't go after whoever triggered the shot because he'd just took a dose of lead," Longarm said.

"Oh, he took after him, all right," Moore explained. "But that crease he got when whoever it was tried to put him down slowed him a bit, so Fred didn't get no place trying to catch up with him. But he's got a pretty good idea who's behind him getting shot."

"Have you got any notion yourself?" Longarm asked. "Seems to me you know a lot about it."

"I got the same idea Fred has. Sully Briggs. Them two don't like each other. Never have and likely never will."

Longarm had already recognized that in stopping to ask directions from the blacksmith he'd stumbled onto what might be a mine of information. He asked, "Now who's this Sully Briggs fellow?"

"Why, Sully's about the biggest man in these parts, to hear him tell it. Owns most of the best land up by the river. Runs cattle and lends money so much that he's talking about opening up a bank, soon as he can get around to it."

"How'd Briggs and Fred happen to get crossways?"

"I don't know of anybody hereabouts that knows why, Marshal Long," Moore replied. His brow wrinkled as he talked. "I guess they must've had some sorta run-in back a ways, because Sully and old Sheriff Collins was right friendly. But Sully's got all that money and land and such, and he kind of figures that makes him a straw boss for the whole town."

"I'd imagine Fred'll know, so I'll ask him," Longarm said. "Now, a minute ago you told me I'll likely find Fred at the sheriff's office. Where might that be?"

"Why, it's at the jail, of course," Moore answered. "In a little town like this one, we can't keep two offices when one serves just about as good."

"That's the same way most little towns do," Longarm said. "And I wouldn't've asked if I had cat eyes that I could see with in the dark."

"Just ride right on through town, past the last house. You look off to the right side of the road, and if it ain't too dark by now you'll see a little rockhouse just a ways off of the road and up on a hill."

"It's dark enough now for 'em to need a lamp, so I don't imagine I'll miss finding it," Longarm said. "And I do thank you for all the help you've been."

"Glad I could help," Moore said. "Stop by again, if I can do anything more."

With a good-bye gesture, Longarm returned to his horse and reined the animal onto the street. A number of the houses where lights had been shining were dark now, but enough of them still remained lighted to let him keep in the middle of the rutted thoroughfare.

He passed several houses, a grocery store, a general store, a butcher's shop, and two or three other commercial buildings, all closed and dark. The only activity on the street was near its end, at a corner where a larger than usual building stood. It was two stories tall and was the biggest that Longarm had seen since leaving the blacksmith shop. Lamplight glowed brightly at the top and bottom of a pair of swinging doors and illuminated the one-word sign above the door: SALOON. The noise of laughter and raised voices within broke the silence that had prevailed along the beginning of the street.

"A tot of good smooth rye'd sure do a lot to settle the dust in your throat, old son," Longarm muttered. "But that's got to wait till after you've done the first part of your job. It ain't likely that saloon there's going to move an inch from where it is, and a sip of good Maryland rye'll taste just as good then as it would right now."

Twitching the reins, Longarm touched the horse's flank with his boot toe. It moved a bit faster, and soon Longarm saw the bulk of a building that stood off the road a short distance beyond the last houses. The building stood on a low crest that rose above the road, on a little ridge. Shades had been drawn at all the windows, but the outlines of the bars that had been fitted to them were silhouetted to give them the appearance of elongated checkerboards. The door in the center of the wall was reinforced with iron straps that repeated the pattern of the windows.

Letting the horse stand, Longarm went to the door and tried the knob. It turned, but he could not open it. He knocked, and after waiting for a few moments without getting a response, he raised his hand to knock again as bolts clicked inside and the door opened. Light flooded out, and Longarm saw the frowning face of his old companion, Fred Carter. He also saw the blue steel of the Colt .45 in Carter's hand.

"You sure run a tight jail, Fred," Longarm said. "You hold a gun on everybody that knocks on your door? Or was you figuring on having some unfriendly company drop in?"

"Longarm!" Carter exclaimed. He shoved his Colt back into its holster and reached for Longarm's extended hand as he went on. "I was hoping Marshal Vail would give you the job of taking Sisson back to Denver, but I didn't feel like I had any right to ask him to."

"He must've read your mind then," Longarm told him as they broke the handshake. "And I reckon you'd just about give up on him sending anybody to pick up that Sisson fellow."

"Not quite," Carter replied. "I figured it'd take some time for you to get here from Denver, but if you hadn't shown up tonight I'd just about made up my mind that I better send Billy another telegram."

"You oughta known I'd be on my way, Fred. Billy ain't one to lallygag on a job like this one."

"He's not, at that. But come on in. We've got a lot of catching up to do. Sisson's the only prisoner I've got here now, and I wasn't about to leave a slippery son of a bitch like him out here at night without somebody to keep an eye on him."

Carter stepped aside and opened the door wider to

72

allow Longarm to enter. Then he went on. "Well, one reason I didn't send Billy another message was because it meant riding over to the Indian Bureau headquarters at the Colville Reservation. That's a full day's ride, north of here, on the other side of the river, but it's where the closest telegraph wire is."

"You mean Billy Vail didn't send you a wire telling you that I was on my way, and for you to look for me?" Longarm asked.

"Maybe he did, but he'd've sent it on the government wire, and it'd have gone to the Indian Bureau office. You and me both know that them pen-pushers in that outfit won't ever win a prize for moving fast."

"Then I'm glad I got here in time to save you the ride. I didn't make as good time as I'd figured I would over what you folks hereabouts calls the Scablands."

"You've got to admit the name fits 'em," Carter said.

"Oh, it does that, all right. How'd you ever get out here and settle down in a place like this?"

"You ought to know, you've done your share of drifting," Carter replied. "And I recall you saying that moving around did you good."

"I don't guess it hurt me none, but after I settled down in Denver, where I'm working out of now, I reckon I've just got too lazy to shift around much. I get enough moving around just going on the cases Billy Vail sends me out to handle."

"Well, come on in," Carter said. As he moved aside to let Longarm enter, he asked, "Billy Vail's doing all right, I suppose?"

"Right as rain," Longarm nodded. "He said give you his best regards."

While they talked, Longarm had been taking stock of

the room they'd entered. It extended across the interior of the building, a long narrow room with small barred windows set high in the wall at each end besides the two larger ones that Longarm had seen from the road. The big chamber was sparsely furnished: a long table in its center, three or four chairs drawn up to it, and a sofa covered by a wrinkled blanket at one end, a rolltop desk at the other. Carter waved toward the table and chairs.

"No, thanks," Longarm said. He began walking slowly around the long narrow room, stamping his feet. As he walked, he said, "I been in the saddle with my knees hoisted up for such a long time that I need to let 'em get good and straight again. But you said your jail's here too, and I don't see no sign of it. Where in hell is it hid?"

"You've just come up the hill from the road," Carter said. "I guess you didn't notice in the dark how this building cuts into the side of the rise." He gestured to the door in the wall beyond the table. "Sheriff Collins was a real smart man. He just had the dirt back there dug out and then they built the back where the jail is into the hole."

Glancing at the wall, Longarm saw that the door in its center was metal-sheathed and its hasp lock was sturdy and over-sized.

Carter went on. "That wall's extra strong, same as the outside ones. Sheriff Collins said he wanted to have a private room in case one was needed, so he had the wall put in to make it that way."

"Sounds like a right good idea to me. But now we've settled down, maybe we better get right on to cases. How long's it going to take for you to hand that Kelly Sisson over to me so's I can start back to Denver?"

"I hope you don't figure to just grab him up and start right on back, Longarm," Carter said. "I been hoping Billy'd send you after Sisson, because I got something in mind that I need to jaw with you about."

"Go ahead and do it then." Longarm paused long enough to take out a cigar and llght it. "The night's young, and I ain't got a thing to do, now that I'm here. But before we start talking about anything else, that blacksmith told me you been hurt, shot."

"Oh, I wouldn't say that," Carter protested. "What I did get was a couple of little grazes that didn't do any more than break my skin." He was rolling up a shirt-sleeve as he replied. Now he extended his left arm and showed a narrow bandage on a reddened patch of skin above his elbow. "There's a streak to match this one on my ribs, but the bullet just went right between them and my arm. It's stopped bothering me any."

Longarm frowned when he looked at the bandage. He said, "That don't look like it's healing awful good, Fred. All the skin around it's too red, and it's still sorta swole up. You had a doctor look at it, didn't you?"

"Sure. Doc Forbes. He said it didn't appear to be real bad, but to look in on him if I had any trouble."

"But you ain't been back?"

"There wasn't much reason. It ain't bothered me till now."

"Was I you, I'd keep an eye on it," Longarm advised. "You wasn't in any sorta face-down then?"

Shaking his head, Carter replied, "I didn't rightly get a look at whoever it was. I was out north of town along the river and the son of a bitch was holed up on a ridge up ahead of me. I hit the dirt fast after that slug went past me. When there wasn't any more shots, I scouted around just a little while, but I didn't pick up a single sign of his trail."

"And you don't know of anybody that's got a grudge against you? Maybe somebody you might've had trouble with?"

"Hells bells, Longarm! It could've been anybody I've ever arrested or kept guard over back there in the jail. I looked over all the ground around the place I figured whoever shot me might be holed up, but that was right after Sheriff Collins was shot and I had to get back here to look after things."

"Well, Fred, I'd say that sure as God made little green apples, there's somebody out to get you." Longarm frowned. "And my bet is they'll try again."

"It's likely," Carter agreed. "But I'm keeping my eyes peeled a little bit better now and trying to remember to look back over my shoulder more than I used to."

"If I could stay over here a spell, I'd be real glad to give you a hand. But I'd have to wire Billy Vail and ask him if it was all right."

"Oh, I'll swear in another deputy pretty soon, pick out one of the fellows I know here in Moses."

"Well, I can stay on here a few days without it bothering me too much," Longarm volunteered.

"And I'd appreciate it if you feel like doing it," Carter replied. "But first let me ask you something." His expression grew very sober now and he spoke a bit more slowly than was his usual habit. "You know me better'n anybody around here does. What kind of a sheriff do you think I'd make?"

"A pretty good one in my book, Fred. You figuring you'll try to get elected to take the job of the one that got killed?"

"I been thinking a lot of doing just that," Carter answered.

"There ain't a thing to stop you from trying, is there?"

Carter did not reply for a moment, then he said soberly, "Longarm, you've known me a long time. Did you ever see me being even a mite fearful to jump into a fracas?"

"I can't say I ever did," Longarm replied. "Why're you asking?"

"Because I've got a feeling that if I was to get elected, it wouldn't be too long before I'd wind up just like Sheriff Collins did. Dead as a doornail."

Chapter 7

Although Longarm was surprised and concerned when
he heard Carter's announcement, he kept his expression
as bland as he would have if he'd been running a bluff
in a poker game. For a moment he did not reply. Then
he said, "I guess you got good reasons for feeling the
way you say you do, Fred."

"I have," Carter replied curtly.

"We worked together on a lot of cases," Longarm went
on. "And I never seen you real buffaloed till now."

"That's likely because I've never run up against a man
like Sully Briggs before."

"You know, Fred, this ain't the first time I've heard
that fellow's name called," Longarm explained. "The
blacksmith out on the other side of town said a few
words about him. They wasn't real kind words either."

"You won't find too many people here who'll say

79

anything good about Sully," Carter said. "I know I sure wouldn't."

"That's what your blacksmith friend I talked to said," Longarm noted. "But he didn't say why. I'd like to know what's your idea about it."

"Well, a lot of the old-timers around here call Briggs a Johnny-come-lately. There's others says he's too uppity, that he's trying to run the town. The psalm-singers don't like him because of that saloon he owns. And I guess there's a few that's just jealous because he keeps on buying more land all the time. They claim he's out to own the whole town and turn it into his own private stamping ground."

"What's your opinion, Fred?"

"Oh, I ain't got much use for him," Carter replied. "But him and old Sheriff Collins was friendly, and I wasn't out to get crossways of my boss, so up until now I've pretty much kept my mouth shut."

"That was just because you didn't want no falling-out between you and the sheriff?"

"I had to go along with the sheriff, Longarm. I guess you'll understand that."

"Reckon I do. But I'm not the sheriff," Longarm pointed out. "Now give me a straight answer, Fred."

"Well, I've only been here a little while, the way Scablanders count time. But from what I've seen of him, I wouldn't say that Sully Briggs is what you'd call likeable. He's one who pokes his nose into everything that's going on, and he wants his own way about everything."

"There's a lot of us who'd like to see things run the way we want 'em to be. Get down to cases, Fred."

"That's what I'm trying to do. First of all, a few

months ago Briggs started buying land claims from folks that couldn't make a go of it out in the Scablands. He still is, and he pushes some real sharp deals with homesteaders that try to sell whatever claim they've got to land they're walking away from."

"Briggs cuts 'em off at the hip pockets, does he?"

"Squeezes 'em down to the last dime," Carter agreed. "Even men that's been working for him a pretty good stretch. When one of his hands gets the idea they want to set up on their own and go to him to draw down their pay, he's mighty particular about finding out where they're aiming to homestead and start up a little ranch of their own. It doesn't happen all the time, but when some of 'em go to buy a piece of land they figure they've got sewed up, they find out Briggs has beat 'em to the deal."

"Now, that sorta sounds to me like he's planning on getting himself the spread of land he'd need for a good-sized cattle ranch," Longarm said when Carter paused.

"What my hunch tells me is he's about ready to do a lot more than just making plans," Carter said quickly. "But I think I mentioned what I've figured, that he's fixing to get real big in these parts. And anybody with half a brain can tell he's working to set up a cattle spread."

"All the signs point that way," Longarm agreed. "But I don't see nothing too wrong about a man wanting to better himself. Do you?"

"If it was anybody but Briggs, I'd agree with you. Now, you know me pretty well, Longarm. You know I don't go off half-cocked."

"Sure. You never was one to do that."

"What I'm getting at is this," Carter went on. "Sheriff Collins is dead and gone. There's got to be a new sheriff voted on, or the governor's going to appoint one. He don't know beans about the Scablands. All he does is squat in his office, and it's way over at the other side of the Territory in Olympia."

"I get the notion you figure that you're the one he'd oughta appoint?"

"Wouldn't you feel the same way, if you were in my shoes?"

"I reckon I would at that," Longarm admitted. "But what makes you think the governor'd call your name for the job?"

"Right now, I haven't got the ghost of an idea what he's likely to do," Carter confessed. "I don't know the governor, nor anything much about him, but a fellow like Briggs will make it his business to do all he can to get the job. If he can't get it for hisself, he'll push for it to go to somebody that's in his pocket."

"And I don't imagine that somebody'd be you," Longarm said drily. After a moment's silence he asked, "You want the sheriff's job pretty bad, don't you, Fred?"

"Sure, I do. Damn it, Longarm, you've been a deputy U.S. marshal for a good spell. Wouldn't you like to be a chief marshal some day?"

"I can't say I would," Longarm replied. A thoughtful frown formed on his face as he spoke. "Me and Billy Vail gets along just fine, but now and then I look at him and think about how he frets all the time, and I'm just as glad it's him doing the fretting instead of me."

"I guess you don't see things of that sort the same way I do," Carter said. "And it's not just the better money I'd be making. I think I'd do a pretty fair job."

"So do I, Fred. If you want that sheriff's job bad enough, you oughta have it. I won't be staying here long enough to give you much of a hand, and I'm a stranger in town to boot, but while I'm here I'll sure do what I can to help you."

"That's what I was hoping you'd say."

"From the way you talk, this Briggs carries a pitchfork and has got horns and a tail with a stinger hanging behind his butt."

"That might not be too strong, Longarm. There's not any love lost between us, but I'll say this much, he could give damn near anybody cards and spades and still hold high-low jack and game."

"Suppose you tell me a little bit more about this Briggs."

"I guess I've told you just about everything I know." Carter paused. "Except that he owns that big saloon in town—you know the one I mean, it's the only one in town, and you'd've passed it on the way out here."

"Well, there's a lot of good decent men that owns saloons too. What makes it so bad for Briggs to have one?"

"Oh, I ain't against saloons, or anything like that," Carter said hastily. "Or even the girls he rents his back rooms to. But I've seen a lot of men that couldn't afford it go broke bucking the gambling games he's got going in it."

"You figure they're crooked then?"

"It's likely, only I never have had a chance to prove it. Old Sheriff Collins was a fine man in a lot of ways, but he was awful damn friendly with Briggs."

"I seen that place when I was riding out here," Longarm said. "But I didn't stop in for a drink, so I wouldn't have much of an idea what goes on inside it." He took out a cigar and lighted it before going on. "I won't argufy that you might be right, but owning a saloon don't give a man a black mark in my book. It ain't against the law. Neither is him getting hands that's worked for him to sign over their claims, but I got to admit it's a right shabby thing to do."

"How about him sending a hired killer to get rid of old Sheriff Collins? And how about me getting shot?"

"You're sure Briggs was behind all that?"

"All I've got to go on was what Sheriff Collins said to me a few days before he was killed. He didn't lay anything right out straight, but I could tell he was fretting over something. I asked him if he was worried, and he sorta grinned and told me he had a real big worry on his mind, but it wasn't anything I could help him with. Then in a day or two he was backshot."

"You know as much about the law as I do," Longarm told Carter. "And the law says you've got to have some evidence to prove that a man you go to arrest really done what you're charging him with."

"Sure. I know all that," Carter replied. "And I'll admit that I don't have any real evidence nor much of a way to get it."

"Maybe you've got a way that you just ain't tumbled to yet."

"Meaning what?"

"Meaning the outlaw you got in the cell behind that door yonder. You say you've got a hunch that Sully Briggs hired Kelly Sisson to murder Sheriff Collins. It seems like to me that Sisson might be able to tell a few tales outa school, if you could just start him talking."

"You think I haven't tried?" Carter asked.

"I didn't mean that. What I'm getting at is that I'm the one who hasn't tried."

84

"What makes you think you'd have a better chance than me?"

"Because I figure I'd have him buffaloed. I've arrested him before. He knows I won't fall for any of his fancy tricks. He's got to be worried, because he knows he'll have just one more chance to get away. And he'll want to keep on my good side, because I'm the one that'll be taking him back to a hangman. He'd likely figure that if he acts like he's folded up I might not watch him too close and he'd have a chance to slip away."

"That's something I hadn't thought about, but I can see how it'd be the case," Carter said. Disappointment crept into his voice as he went on. "I was halfway hoping you'd feel like staying here long enough to rest up before starting back. I could sure use some help for a few days, until I sorta get my feet on the ground in this new job I've dropped into."

"Don't get edgy, Fred. I don't aim to turn my back to you."

"That sure makes me feel a lot better. What can I do to get you started off?"

"Since you're asking, I'll get to what I'm driving at. A minute or so ago, when you said something about that saloon Briggs owns here in town, I got some sorta ghost of a notion about where to start in."

"A notion about finding a way to get around Sully Briggs? Now, that I'd like to see."

"Let's don't count chickens before they're hatched," Longarm said. "I'm still trying to figure all of it out."

"What's your idea?"

"Let me think about it a little while before I trot it out for you," Longarm suggested. "But while I'm thinking, I better be tending to the case that I'm really here for. I don't guess you'd mind me talking to Kelly Sisson?"

"Not a bit, Longarm. When you come down to it, he's your prisoner, even if he's in my jail right now."

Carter was getting to his feet as he spoke. He stepped over to the rolltop desk and took a key ring from the drawer. Longarm joined him as he walked toward the door leading to the cells and unlocked it. When the metal-sheathed door swung open, the room beyond it was blackly forbidding.

Striking a match, Carter cupped it in his hand as he stepped inside. The feeble glow did not light the area away from the door. Then he touched the match to the wick of a kerosene lamp on a shelf behind the door. After a momentary flickering the glow from the lamp grew steady and lighted the short row of three barred doors that stretched across the narrow room. Longarm followed Carter by a step. He came through the door just as bed-clothes rustled in the shadowed area at the rear of a cell and a sleepy voice broke the silence.

"What the hell's going on? If I've slept out a night, I sure don't feel like it."

"Why, you've got a real important visitor, Sisson," Carter said. "He's come a long way to get you, and the least you can do is get up and say hello to him."

Longarm hardly recognized Sisson as the outlaw pressed his face against the cell door's bars. The renegade's cheeks and chin were covered by a thick touseled beard; only his nose, his gleaming eyes, and his forehead were visible.

"Well, damned if it ain't Longarm!" Sisson exclaimed. "It seems like a year ago that they said somebody'd be coming to haul me back to the States. I didn't even think it might be you."

"Oh, it's me, all right," Longarm assured him. "And soon as I can manage, we'll be starting back to the prison you busted out of, so you better be making up your mind to do some traveling."

Sisson grunted, then he said, "Take your time. I'd liefer stay here than go back, but it don't look like I got much to say about it."

"You haven't," Longarm told him. Turning to Carter, he went on. "I've seen all I need to. Let's get back where we can breathe some fresher air and give him a chance to think about what he's got coming to him when he gets back to where I'll be taking him."

As Longarm stepped to the door where Carter was waiting, Sisson called, "Listen to me, Long! If you think I'm going to give you any rest after we get started back, you sure better think again! Because I ain't got a thing to lose, and I'd damn sure rather die out in the open than dangling at the end of a noose! Now don't say I ain't—"

Sisson's shouted threats were cut off by the slamming of the door as Longarm and Carter entered the office area and the deputy swung the door shut and locked it. He turned to Longarm and shook his head.

"I'm glad he's your prisoner instead of mine," the deputy said. "Because I've seen enough of him while we've been holding him for you to know he meant what he was saying."

"I don't misdoubt it for a minute," Longarm replied. "But I've handled a few others that was just about as mean. I ain't perzactly looking for no picnic, but I'll manage. Now, if you'll wait just a minute while I go get my bedroll off of my horse, I'll be more than ready to get myself a little shut-eye."

"You take the cot then," Carter suggested. "I'll make do on the floor tonight."

"You know I ain't going to take away your bed, Fred," Longarm protested. "You're hurt and I'm so tired I could drop off to sleep on a pile of cobblestones in a boiler factory. Now, you sleep in your regular bed and I'll fix myself up and be dead to the world in about two minutes."

"Well, if you're sure—"

"I've told you the way it's going to be," Longarm replied. "Now let's go on and get ourselves settled without argufying over who'll sleep where."

Carter was already half asleep when Longarm returned with his own bedroll. Wearier than he liked to admit, even to himself, Longarm dropped off to sleep within minutes after levering out of his boots and pulling his blanket up around his shoulders.

When the sound of low groans roused Longarm and he opened his eyes to the room's pitch-darkness, he had no idea how long he'd been asleep. Even before he was fully awake he was reaching for the butt of his Colt that lay on the floor behind him. Then, as he heard another moan and realized that it had come from Carter, Longarm sat up in his bedroll.

"Fred?" he called. "You having trouble, or just a bad dream?"

"I'm afraid it's trouble," Carter replied. His voice was strained and thin. "I'm swelling up all around where that bullet scraped me, my arm and my side both. And I'm starting to hurt."

Kicking his blankets off his legs, Longarm stood up as he said, "I didn't like the looks of 'em, but I figured you'd been to the doctor and he'd told you not to worry."

"He did."

"Sure," Longarm said. "But gangrene lays quiet a spell before it jumps and starts puffing up."

He was flicking his thumbnail across a match head as he spoke. The match flared and before its flame reached his fingertips he'd located and lighted the lamp on the table. Even at a glance he could tell that his friend was in more trouble than he realized. Carter was sitting up on the cot, his wounded arm draped across his knees. A flush showed on his face and the upper portion of the arm was an even darker red. It was also swollen, bulging up around the edges of the narrow bandage.

"I reckon your side's swole up too?" Longarm asked.

"Some. At least, it feels like it is. Not as bad as my arm, though."

"You feel too sick to fork a horse?"

"A horse?" Carter frowned.

"Sure. That damn bullet hole's gone gangrene now. You need a doctor. And right away, soon as we can get to one." Longarm had already pulled on his trousers and was stepping into his boots. He went on. "I'd go get that one you told me about, but by the time I found his place and he got ready to start back here we'd've wasted a lot of time."

"I don't feel too bad to ride," Carter said. "Provided you give me a little bit of help."

"That's just what I aim to do. And the quicker we get to that doctor's place, the better off you'll be."

"Your friend Carter's a very lucky man," young Doctor Forbes told Longarm as he came out of his little surgery.

"I've put poultices on his arm and side, and with luck they'll draw out the infection that's started."

"You mean he'll be all right then?"

"It's quite likely. You did the right thing in bringing him out here at once. The infection hasn't spread far from the wounds, and I'm certain that the medicine I've used will kill it very quickly. But I won't be able to do much more right now. A bullet-scrape is always a tricky thing to treat."

"So I been told. I don't reckon there's anything much I can do by staying around, is there?"

Forbes shook his head. "Not a thing, Marshal Long. I've given him a sleeping draught, and until . . . oh, sometime this afternoon . . . I won't know just how he'll be getting along. But if there's anything you can do in the meantime, I'll let you know. I suppose you'll be at the sheriff's office? Carter seemed anxious about a prisoner in the jail there."

"That's an outlaw killer he arrested," Longarm said. "I told you I work outa the U.S. marshal's office in Denver, and that prisoner got away from a federal prison. That's why I come here, to get him back where he's due to be hanged. I'll be at the jail if you need to get hold of me."

"So I understand," the doctor said. "If I should need you for anything, I'll send you a message. If you don't hear from me, drop by late today."

"I'll do just that," Longarm replied. "And seeing as we left the jail in a sorta hurry, I better get back there and make sure everything's all right."

Though it seemed to Longarm that the night had been unusually long, the sky was still dark when he got outside. He mounted, looped the reins of the horse Carter had ridden over the pommel of his saddle, and started toward the town. As he rode closer to it he saw that the lights of all the houses were dark now. The only gleam of brightness came from the saloon he'd passed on his way to the sheriff's office.

"Old son," he muttered under his breath, "you had a real long day and one that was pretty busy. What you need right now is a good swallow of rye to perk you up before you get back to bed."

Reining in at the saloon's hitch rail, he wrapped the reins of his horse around it and went inside.

Chapter 8

Pushing through the batwings, Longarm headed for the bar. He glanced around the saloon as he crossed the floor. A white-aproned barkeeper was leaning on a corner of the glistening mahogany bar that stretched across the rear of the cavernous interior. He had an elbow propped on the bar and appeared to be a bit more than half asleep.

At a table in one corner of the room four or five men were engrossed in a poker game. At another, nearer the center, a solitary drunk was sprawled out facedown. He was obviously unconscious; his head was turned sideways, his mouth half-open, and his arms draped limply across the tabletop. At the back of the room Longarm could see two people sitting at a table that was in an alcove created by the stairway. They were in the deep shadow created by the upslanting stairs, and all that Longarm could make out was the glint or two from a satin skirt which told him one of the dimly seen forms was a woman.

His boot heels thunking on the floor of the big room, Longarm crossed it and stopped at the bar. The barkeeper did not rouse until Longarm dropped a silver cartwheel on the mahogany. Its tingling ringing brought the man out of his somnolence. He stood up, glanced along the bar, and shuffled along until he reached Longarm.

Fully awake by now, he asked, "What's your pleasure, stranger?"

"Tom Moore rye, if you've got any of it. If you ain't, I can do with John Thompson, or even Gilson in a pinch."

"I can sure tell you're a stranger to the Scablands." The barkeeper smiled. "Folks around here ain't real choosy about what they drink, long as it stays down after they swallow it."

"I like to enjoy while I'm swallowing," Longarm replied. "But if you're short of good rye whiskey—"

"Now, I didn't say that," the barkeeper broke in. "It just happens I've got a bottle of Moore that's never even been opened. I'll be right glad to step back in the stockroom and trot it out for you." Raising his voice, he called, "Lexie! Come keep this gent company for a minute or two, I got to go to the stockroom and dig up a special bottle for him!"

With a rustle of her skirt, the woman who'd been sitting in the obscurity of the nook stood up and came to stand beside Longarm.

"It's nice to see a fresh face," she said. "In a little town like this especially."

"Well, you're one in this little town that I'd say has got a pretty face to look at," he replied.

"Why, thank you." She smiled. "I hope you're not just traveling through, the way most folks are when they get into the Scablands."

Longarm was taking in her features as she talked. Her hair was a fluffy blond roll arched over her forehead and gathered into a pouf at the back. She had light thin eyebrows above deep blue eyes, high heavily rouged cheekbones, an acquiline nose that was just a bit too long, full lips, and a chin that was adequate but could have been a bit wider. Her low-cut satin dress had been fitted to pull her bulging breasts together and emphasize their fullness.

"You're new in town," she said. Her voice was low-pitched and husky. "I guess you heard Pleas call my name. In case you didn't, it's Lexie."

"Oh, I heard him all right. Pleased to make your acquaintance, Lexie. My name's Long, Custis Long. And you're right about me being new here. I just rode in yesterday evening."

"And if you're like most people that stop in Moses you're likely to ride out tomorrow."

"Not hardly. My business brought me here, so I won't be leaving till it's finished."

"Then you'll be—" She broke off as the barkeeper returned, carrying a dust-crusted bottle, then said as she moved away, "Next time you stop in, you won't be a stranger."

"Oh, as long as I know I can get good rye whiskey, you'll see me here now and again."

With a nod of farewell, Lexie turned to go back to the dark corner where she'd been sitting. While Longarm was chatting with Lexie the barkeeper had been wiping the dust off the bottle of Tom Moore and extracting its cork. He slid a shot glass in front of Longarm and lifted the whiskey bottle.

"A man that drinks Tom Moore ain't likely to want it anyway but straight," he commented. "Am I right?"

"You sure are," Longarm agreed, watching as the man filled the glass. Lifting it, Longarm swallowed half its contents and replaced the glass on the bar while he fished out a cigar and lighted it.

"Business bring you here?" the barkeeper asked, exercising the prerogative of his trade to make such inquiries of strangers.

"I guess you'd call it that," Longarm answered after he'd taken his cigar from his mouth.

"Wait a minute! I got a hunch I know who you are, now. I heard some talk about a federal lawman coming after that fellow Deputy Sheriff Carter's got in his lockup. I bet you're him!"

Though he would have preferred to keep such details out of their conversation, Longarm's ingrained habit of refusing to lie unless duty required him to do so was too strong for him to break.

"You'd win the bet, supposing we'd made one," he said. "My name's Long. Deputy U.S. marshal outa the Denver office."

"I've heard Fred Carter call your name a time or two," the barman went on. "You and him are old friends, he says."

"We are. Fred's not along with me now because he got shot up a bit—but I guess you'd know more about that than I do."

"Oh, I know about it, all right. But he looked to be in pretty good shape the last time he was in here."

"You'll know he got grazed then?" When the barman

96

nodded Longarm went on. "Well, the graze give him some sort of trouble this evening, so I taken him out to the doctor's."

"Now, I'm sure sorry about that."

"Not anymore sorry than me," Longarm said. "I was hoping all I'd have to do was pick up that killer he's holding and take him back to Colorado, where a hangman's waiting for him."

"Are you saying he'll get hanged without being tried first?"

"Oh, he's been tried and judged guilty, all regular and proper and according to the book," Longarm replied. He finished his drink and returned the glass to the bar, pointing to the freshly opened bottle of Tom Moore to indicate that he was ready for his glass to be refilled.

"Well, now." The barkeeper frowned, picking up the bottle to pour Longarm's drink. "That'd have to be the fellow Fred Carter brought in just after Sheriff Collins got killed. If I ain't mixed up, his name's Kelly Sissons, but he was passing under another one here. And I recall hearing folks say that he's a right bad one."

"Bad enough for a jury to find him guilty on a murder charge and a judge sentence him to hang," Longarm pointed out. He picked up the filled glass and took another swallow of the pungent rye whiskey.

"He ain't the only bad one hiding in the Scablands. Maybe that's one reason why folks ain't making no rush to file on land there since the gov'mint opened it up for homesteading a while back."

"Might be," Longarm agreed. Draining his glass he put it down on the bar and pushed the cartwheel he'd dropped there earlier across the polished mahogany as he went on. "I got to be moseying along. But keep that

Tom Moore handy, because I'll likely be back for a tot now and then."

"Anytime you're passing by," the barkeeper said. He picked up the coin, turned to the till to make change, and dropped a half-dollar and two dimes on the bar in front of Longarm as he went on, "I reckon you know good whiskey like Tom Moore costs a nickel more than our regular bar liquor."

"And worth it too," Longarm replied as he scooped up the coins and dropped them in his pocket. "You won't hear me—" He broke off as he saw Lexie rise from her seat in the shadows and start toward him.

"Excuse me, Marshal Long," she said, "but—"

"Now, how'd you tumble to the fact that I'm a marshal?" Longarm asked. "I recall telling it to the barkeep just now, except that I don't remember I told you when we was talking a minute ago. Not that it's any secret, a course, but I'm a mite curious."

"There's no secret to how I learned it either," Lexie replied. "Over where I've been sitting you can hear just about everything that's said along the bar."

"And you and the fellow with you've been listening all along to what me and the barkeep was talking about?"

"Please don't get upset or angry," Lexie said. "When it's quiet the way it is now, somebody in that corner hears everything whether they want to or not. But that's not why I came over here. The man I've been sitting with would like to have a word with you."

"I don't guess he said about what?" When Lexie shook her head Longarm went on. "I'll stop and see, then."

With a nod to Lexie, Longarm walked over to the man sitting beneath the stairway. In the gloom of the corner recess he could barely make out the man's features. All that he could see was that the sitting stranger was big and husky.

Longarm said, "The young lady told me you'd like to have a word or two with me."

"I thought it might be a good idea," the stranger replied. His words sounded slurred, and Longarm understood why when he saw the lowered level of the whiskey bottle on the table. His voice a bit blurred, the man went on, indicating the bottle. "Pour yourself a drink."

"Thanks all the same," Longarm replied. "But I had as much as I wanted for the evening."

"I noticed Lexie didn't tell you my name. It's Sully Briggs."

"I've heard you mentioned a time or two," Longarm said.

"That's likely, here in Moses," Briggs said. He'd refilled his glass. Now he swallowed a sip before going on, "Just about everybody around knows me. And I've heard your nickname called too, Marshal Long. If I'm not mistaken, you're the one they call Longarm."

"It's sorta got hung on me," Longarm explained. "But I'm a mite surprised you've heard it called, seeing as I only got here such a little spell ago."

"There's damned little I don't hear about here in Moses," Briggs said. There was no boastfulness in the tone of his voice, and without pausing he asked, "How's Fred Carter getting along out at Doc Forbes's place?"

Groping for the reason that he was sure lay behind Briggs's question, Longarm replied, "The doctor says he'll be all right, but he's going to be under the weather a little while."

"You'll be staying until he's recovered, I suppose?"

"Oh, sure. I'm just on my way back to his office right now. I promised him I'd sorta keep an eye on things till he's fixed up and gets back to his job again."

Briggs was taking another swallow of whiskey. He nodded, and after he'd downed the liquor he went on. "I saw you were a bit surprised when Lexie told you I wanted to talk with you. Now, you don't know much about me, Long, but I've heard quite a bit about you."

"Even out here in the Scablands?" Longarm asked.

"I haven't lived in the Scablands all my life. I did my share of traveling before I settled down. But that's neither here nor there. I've got just one question I want to ask you, and I'll thank you right now for giving me a straight answer."

"I ain't one to beat around a bush myself. What's your question?"

Briggs deferred his reply until he'd drained the shot glass he held. Then he tilted his head toward Longarm and asked, "How'd you like to be a very, very rich man?"

When Longarm heard Briggs's question, its totally unexpected nature surprised him so completely that he could find no immediate reply. He was a veteran of surprises of almost every kind, from a showdown with an outlaw to a pat winning poker hand, but the one he'd just received was so complete that for a moment he simply sat staring at the man across the table.

"You don't have to be all that surprised," Briggs went on when Longarm did not reply at once. "I'm not joshing you. What I'm asking is how you'd like to be richer than Morgan or Rockefeller or Carnegie or any of those other big moguls back East."

"Well, now," Longarm said at last, "that sounds like a pretty good-sized order. I reckon I'd live through it, but I don't see how you figure to make somebody else rich unless you make yourself a lot richer."

"Of course," Briggs replied. His voice was slurred, flat, and almost expressionless. "That's exactly what I've got in mind."

"Where's all this money you're talking about going to come from? I'd say for sure it'd have to be honest money, because it's the only kind that's any good. And that kind of money ain't always easy to come by."

"Land's going to get me the money," Briggs replied quickly.

"Honest or not, land don't make money by itself," Longarm objected. "It's how it's used that makes folks money."

"You're wrong there, Long. Money's made by selling land, not using it."

"And what happens when you run out of land?"

"You never do, if you work your scheme right," Briggs said. "You sell the same land over and over again."

"That sounds like it'd be a good scheme," Longarm observed. "Except I can't see how you figure to do it."

"Have you ever bought land?" Briggs challenged. "Or homesteaded it?"

"I can't say I have. Now, my family back in West Virginia homesteaded when I was a younker, and when they'd farmed it for seven years, which was as long as the government said they had to, they got a deed saying it was theirs, and nobody could take it away from 'em."

"But if they hadn't put in seven years, the land would've gone back to the government," Briggs said quickly. He lifted his empty glass, frowned, and replaced it on the table. "It could've been claimed by anybody then, but whoever did that would've had to start all over and farm it another seven years. And if that next bunch didn't make it, it would've gone to somebody else."

"I reckon I got to agree to that," Longarm noted. "But I still don't see how you figure to come out."

"You don't think along the same lines I do," Briggs told him. "Let me tell you something, Marshal Long. What's out in the Scablands isn't farmland. There'll never be enough water on it for farming. It's ranchland, and I'm a rancher. I intend to get my hands on every inch of land I can out there and have me the biggest ranch anywhere."

"I wish you well," Longarm said. "But I got to admit I don't see why you're telling me all this."

"You need to know what I'm planning to do," Briggs replied. "You still haven't heard my proposition."

"Suppose you tell me then. If I like what I hear, I might listen to some more of your palaver."

"Right now, I've got more than twenty claims that I've bought back off people that filed out in the Scablands and found out they couldn't make a go of it. But that's too slow, I've got to wait too long."

"Wait for what?" Longarm asked.

"More land, of course. I don't suppose you'd know much about this part of the Territory, but there's a stretch of land between two rivers north of here that I've got my eye on. It's pretty much level and not as rocky as most of that country up there. Good water, two little lakes on it, and a few creeks. All that land's going to be mine, Long."

"Remembering what I seen on my map, that's a right big chunk of Washington Territory," Longarm said. "It's sure a lot more'n you can claim as a homestead. I don't see—"

"I do!" Briggs broke in. He was wrapped up in his subject now, his eyes glistening as much from excitement as from the whiskey he'd drunk. "I'll get a lot of people to file a lot more claims. When they can't make a go of it and get ready to drift off, I'll give 'em a few dollars travel money for their claims."

"What if they don't drift?" Longarm asked. "And why're you telling me all this?"

"If they get mulish and try to hang on, I know a lot of ways to change their minds," Briggs boasted. "Besides, that's where you'd come in. From what I've heard about you, there's not much you can't do with a sixgun. I'll need a man like you, a gunfighter, a killer."

"Hold on now!" Longarm objected. "I ain't neither one!"

"That's not what I've heard." Briggs was genuinely excited now. "You've killed and you've been in gunfights, I know that for sure!"

"And I ain't saying I haven't shot men, or killed a few," Longarm replied. "But I'm a lawman, and them I've had to shoot was out to kill me. There ain't one of 'em that didn't have a gun in his hand throwing down on me before I ever let off a shot!"

"So you say!" Briggs exclaimed. His face was flushed now and his eyes goggling widely. "But I'll tell you some—" He came to an abrupt stop and shook his head. "Maybe we better not talk any longer, not right now."

"I'm as ready to stop as you are," Longarm said, getting to his feet. "And you've told me enough so's I know I ain't interested in whatever your proposition is. I'll just say good night now, and be on my way."

Without waiting for Briggs to reply, Longarm stood

up and walked to the door. He looked back only once, but in the badly lighted corner he'd just left, he could see Briggs only dimly. He'd fallen back in his chair, and the barkeep was hurrying toward him. The men who'd been in the saloon had left while he and Briggs were talking, and Lexie was nowhere to be seen. Freeing his horse from the hitch rail, Longarm swung into the saddle and started toward the sheriff's office.

In the east the first light of false dawn was beginning to give the sky a tinge of gray when Longarm reached the squat little building. He tethered his horse, took off its saddle, and went inside. In the gloom of the outer office he could just make out the details of the room's furnishings. Deciding that both he and Kelly Sisson could wait a while for breakfast, Longarm went to the touseled bed. Stopping only long enough to take off his boots, he dropped onto the cot and was asleep almost the moment his head touched the rumpled pillow.

Chapter 9

Longarm was roused by the thuds of booted feet stamping on the floor accompanied by the muffled sound of Kelly Sisson's angry voice beyond the closed door leading to the jail cells. He sat up in bed, looking around the sunlight-flooded sheriff's office. Then as Sisson renewed his calls and the thunking started again, Longarm swung his feet to the floor and without waiting to shove them into his boots, padded over to the door between the office and the cells.

"Damn it, Long! What're you trying to do, starve a man to death?" Sisson demanded when Longarm swung the door open. "Half the day's gone by and you ain't brought me my breakfast yet!"

"Just hold your horses a minute or two," Longarm advised the outlaw. "And don't go getting feisty with me. You'd best remember that you're the one in the jail, and I'm the one in charge. Tie down that wagging tongue of yours, and I'll get you some grub fixed up. Just wait till I can step into my boots and roust around and find out what's left in here to feed you."

Longarm explored the supply cabinet, and found nothing but a few crusts of dry bread and the bone of a cured ham bared to within an inch of the shank's end. He shaved off the fat-crusted meat, gathered up the largest pieces of the hard dried bread, and took the plate in to the cell area.

"You call that a breakfast?" Sisson demanded when he saw the plate. "Hell's bells, Long! Them scraps and shavings wouldn't fill a man's hollow tooth!"

"They'll keep you from starving till I can do better," Longarm told the protesting prisoner as he tilted the plate to slide it through the bars of the cell door. "And I didn't hold back nothing from you that was fit to eat, even if I'm as hungry as you are."

"Not likely! All there is for me to do is look at these damn blank walls and wish I was someplace else," Sisson grunted. He picked up a sliver of the ham and started chewing on it.

"Now, I've got to eat too," he reminded Sisson. "And I've given you the only grub there is out here. Just as quick as I can shave and look decent, I'll go to town and get something more, but right now this is all there is."

Sisson did not reply, he was already picking up pieces of ham and bread and cramming them into his mouth. Longarm went back into the office, closing the door of the cell area and locking it behind him. He glanced around at the office, where the signs of his hasty departure with Fred Carter the previous night were still very much in evidence.

"You got a job on your hands to clean things up a little bit, old son," he said aloud. "But that can wait till you see how Fred's getting along today. Might be the doc'll let him come back to work. Then you got to get in a stock of grub and eat some breakfast yourself. And the sooner you get moving, the better off you'll be."

Shrugging into his shirt and smoothing his wrinkled trousers as best he could, Longarm pushed his feet into his boots, strapped on his gunbelt, and went outside. The brightness of the cloudless day and the ripple of fresh breeze lifted his spirits. The horse was already saddled. He levered himself to its back and started for Dr. Forbes's little office.

"I'll sure be glad when I'm well enough to get outa here, so I can hold up my end of things," Carter told Longarm after hearing about the night's developments. "That damned Sully Briggs acts like a wild man when he gets his head set on doing something. But if you've got wind enough left to carry through awhile, I'll be around to help you soon as the doc lets me go."

"Has he told you when that'll be?" Longarm asked. "It ain't that I'm hurting, but you know the territory and the folks here a lot better'n I do."

"All Doc Forbes has done is shake his head and say tomorrow or the next day."

"That's just how he done me when I asked him how much longer you'd have to stay on here. I reckon he figured if it was good enough for you, it'd be good enough for me," Longarm said. He stood up. "Now I better mosey back to town. I been here long enough, what with Doc Forbes being nice enough to feed me my breakfast."

Outside in the early morning sunshine Longarm swung into the saddle and reined the horse toward town. He'd almost reached the road-fork when the animal broke its gait and started limping. Longarm did not need to dismount to find out what was wrong. He knew the trouble was a loose shoe.

Letting his horse set its own increasingly ragged pace, Longarm turned it down the town's only real street, heading for the blacksmith shop. Moses was coming to life. There were saddled horses and a wagon or two in front of all three of the stores, and a few early morning loafers on the steps of Sully Briggs's saloon. Longarm heard the clangs of metal on metal even before he reached the smithy. Turning toward its yawning open door, he dropped his crippled mount's reins and went inside.

"Well, Marshal Long!" Ben Moore greeted him, looking up from the reddened but rapidly darkening link he'd just put into a chain. "I see you remembered my invitation to drop in when you were close by. Sit down and make yourself at home. I generally knock off for a little breather when I've finished a job."

"Thanks, but I been sitting too much," Longarm replied. "And this ain't just a friendly visit. I got a horse outside with a loose shoe it's close to throwing."

"That's easy to fix," Moore said. "It won't take me but a few minutes—well, maybe a little bit longer—to fit a new shoe onto his hoof. I've found out that mostly it's better to do that than it is trying to tighten up a worn-out one."

"You figure for me to wait while you're doing the job?"

"Unless you're in a mighty big hurry to get someplace. If you are, I keep a couple of horses out in back of the

108

smithy to lend folks that can't wait while I'm shoeing theirs."

"I got more'n enough time. I'll just sit and watch."

"Rest yourself then. I'll get started right away."

While Longarm watched, the blacksmith led the horse up to the anvil. He pulled out the loose nail with a pair of pinchers, then levered the loose shoe free. He held it out for Longarm to inspect, pointing to the nail-channel along the horseshoe's front curve.

"Your nag's thrown one nail, and if you were watching when I took the shoe off, you could see how loose the others are. I'll just shape a new shoe and put it on, if you've got the time to wait."

"Guess I better take the time," Longarm said. "Because tomorrow or the next day I figure to be starting back with the prisoner I come for."

"I've been wondering myself what's going to happen to him," Moore replied without looking up from his work. He'd already taken several horseshoes from a keg. Now he hunkered down beside the horse, propped its shoeless hoof on one of his knees, and tried to match the hoof's curve with one of the new horseshoes. "You know, a few folks have got the idea that fellow's going to be hanged here in Moses."

"There's a lot of 'em who don't understand how the law reads," Longarm said.

"Oh, they'll catch on when the word gets around that you'll be taking him back to where he was tried and sentenced," Moore said. He'd now found a horseshoe with the proper size, and pushed it into the bed of glowing coals in the forge. Stepping to the bellows, he started pumping them. Raising his voice to carry over the hissing of the brightening coals, he said, "You're sure right about people not understanding the law. If they did, there wouldn't be so many that get fleeced by that damned Sully Briggs."

Longarm saw an opportunity and took advantage of it. He said noncommittally, "It sounds to me like you don't care much for Briggs."

"I don't. In my book he's like a lot of other rich men, just a mean bully. He cheats a lot of poor devils that buy land from him on a time-lease too. I've helped a few of them who'd had to leave when he foreclosed on notes they'd signed and gotten behind in paying. It's not easy to start farming from scratch in the Scablands, Marshal Long, not when you're buying land from a greedy rascal like Sully Briggs."

"Well, I got to admit, I didn't cotton to him myself when I met him last night."

Moore nodded but did not reply. While they were talking he'd lifted the glowing red horseshoe in a pair of long-handled pinchers, and was swiveling to the anvil close by. He picked up the forging hammer and began shaping the hot metal with quick sure blows, shifting it swiftly now and then to the anvil's beak to hammer it into the contours of the old shoe's curve.

During the few minutes he worked, the shape of the new shoe altered subtly. Lifting the tongs to hold it above the old one, Moore nodded with satisfaction when he saw that the contour of the two shoes matched perfectly. He plunged the new shoe into a bucket of water beside the forge and stepped through the cloud of steam rising from it.

"Another five minutes," he told Longarm. "Just long enough to trim your nag's hoof and nail on the new shoe and you can be moving again."

110

"I ain't in all that big of a hurry," Longarm said. "There's just that Sisson fellow out in the jail, and he won't be going no place for a while."

Moore made short work of driving the horseshoe nails into their slots. As he laid his hammer aside and let the horse's hoof drop to the floor Longarm asked, "How much do I owe you for the job?"

"A dollar'll cover it," Moore replied. "You ought not have any trouble with it, but if you do, come on back and I'll fix it without it costing you a penny."

"Looks to me like you done a pretty good job," Longarm said. "But if it needs anything more, I'll sure be back."

With a good-bye wave to Ben Moore, Longarm mounted and reined the horse back into the road, heading toward town. The day was well along now, the hitch rails in front of the small stores almost deserted. On one of the stores the words GROCERIES & MEATS reminded Longarm of the jail's food shortage. Pulling up, he stopped at the store long enough to buy a dozen airtights of beans and another of tomatoes, a cured ham and a large chunk of cheese, as well as several boxes of crackers, and to arrange for the food to be delivered to the sheriff's building.

Glancing at the morning sun as he remounted, Longarm resumed his progress to the sheriff's office. He reached the saloon and for a moment considered stopping for a drink, but the thought of another unpleasant run-in with Sully Briggs caused him to reconsider. He was riding on past the building when Lexie burst through the swinging doors and called to him.

"Longarm! Aren't you going to stop and say good morning?"

"Why, I had it in mind, Lexie. But I got to admit I didn't have no hankering to waste my time having another brush with your boss, so I just decided to go on about my business."

"If that's all that was stopping you, there's nothing to worry about," Lexie told him. "Sully left last night just a little while after you did. He said he had some important business to take care of at the place he's working on up at Whistling Rock. Usually when he goes out to the Scablands he'll be away for a day or two, maybe even a week."

"Well, if he ain't going to be around, then I'll just come in and take your invitation to have me an eye-opener. That fine Maryland rye'll go down real good about this time of day."

Swinging out of his saddle, Longarm tossed the reins over the hitch rail and followed Lexie into the saloon. There were no customers at the bar or tables and no bartender behind the long stretch of mahogany.

"Ain't it awful quiet for as late in the day as it is?" Longarm asked.

"No, it's pretty much the same every morning," she said. "There'll be a few early drinkers, but they're gone by noon, then a few come in at noon, but all they want is a quick drink before they have to go back to work. Late in the day's when the business really starts in here."

"Then it looks like we'll have the place to ourselves."

"Not quite," Lexie replied. "The barkeep's in the back room there, filling his bottles." While she was explaining, Lexie had gone behind the bar and picked up the bottle of Tom Moore as well as two shot glasses. Now she stepped around the end of the bar. "I'm just in the mood to join you in having a sip of this, Marshal Long. I don't touch liquor very often, and—well, what I'm really getting around to is inviting you to come upstairs with me where we can enjoy our drink without anybody disturbing us."

"That's an invitation I can't say no to," Longarm told her. "If it pleases you, it pleases me."

Lexie nodded and led the way to the stairs. Longarm followed her up the steps and along a door-lined corridor. She opened one of the doors and stood aside to allow him to enter, then followed him in. A double bed dominated the small chamber; a chair and a washstand were the only other furniture in the narrow room. As Longarm turned to look at her, Lexie smiled.

"You're not very surprised, are you?" she asked.

"I sorta figured you might have something besides a drink in mind," he replied. "Ladies generally do, when they invite a man into their bedroom."

Lexie had stepped to the table and was putting the bottle of Tom Moore on it. She turned back to Longarm to say, "This isn't my bedroom, but it's a lot handier. You know from last night that I'm supposed to be Sully's girl, and I hope that won't make any difference one way or the other."

"Being a man's girl don't mean he owns you," Longarm told her. "I don't feel like a woman oughta belong to anybody."

"I'm glad I wasn't mistaken in my judgment of you," Lexie said as she filled the two small glasses. She handed one to Longarm. "Since we're being honest with each other, I don't mind telling you that I stay with Sully because he's a rich man. If his schemes work out, he'll likely be even richer. But he drinks too much and he's gone too much. I need a lot more than he can give me."

113

Longarm was neither surprised nor repulsed by Lexie's frankness. He'd encountered other women who'd told him much the same thing. He raised his glass and they tossed off their drinks. Lexie put her glass on the small nightstand and stepped up to him and tilted her head back. Longarm was ready to accept her invitation. His erection was already beginning and the subtle perfume that she brought with her was having its effect.

Wrapping her in his arms, Longarm bent to meet her lips and they clung together in a long embrace. As their tongues entwined Lexie slipped a hand between them to grope for and find his bulging erection. Longarm shifted to make her search easier. She grasped him and caressed the burgeoning shaft for a moment before twisting to break away from his arms.

"We're wasting time," she said. "Why're we standing here while there's a bed waiting for us?"

Turning, Lexie gestured to the line of hooks and eyes that ran up the back of her dress. Longarm fumbled them free and she shrugged to send the dress rippling to the floor.

"You're slow," she said, spreading her arms and displaying her nude body. Against soft snow-white skin the pebbled tips of her breasts swayed invitingly and her pubic brush was a golden vee. She went on. "You helped me, so it's my turn to help you now."

Longarm took off his gunbelt and laid the belt with its holstered Colt on the nightstand while Lexie's fingers twinkled along the line of buttons from his shirt to the crotch of his trousers. While she was undoing the buttons Longarm levered out of his boots, shrugged out of his shirt, and kicked away his trousers. Lexie fell back on the bed and spread her thighs invitingly. Longarm kneeled between them and as Lexie placed him he dropped and drove into her.

She met his deep penetration with her upthrust hips and sighed in a faltering tremolo that ended in a small shriek of delight as he filled her. For a few moments Longarm lay motionless, buried fully, then Lexie began to rotate her hips slowly. Longarm caught her rhythm and started thrusting, slowly and deliberately, prolonging for both of them the mounting sensations that his slow caresses were creating. Now and then he stopped his steady penetration while Lexie tried to pull him in more deeply by locking her ankles behind his back and jerking her hips upward.

Minutes ticked away until Lexie's body started to tremble. Longarm thrust deeply and stopped, holding himself fully engulfed by her. Lexie twisted her hips and brought them up, trying to pull him into her more deeply, but Longarm let his full weight press on her. Though she twisted her hips again and again, he did not resume thrusting until Lexie's small shudders stopped.

As they died away, she opened her eyes and gazed up at him and asked, "Are you a man or a miracle, Longarm? Because you certainly know how to treat a woman, making her feel like she wants to let go and hold back all at the same time."

"Let go then," he told her.

"I—I want to, but somehow I don't."

"Which do you want the most?"

"Both!" she said decisively. "If you're ready, I am."

"Oh, I got a little more steam left," he assured her. "You just let go when you feel like it and we'll see what happens."

"Go on and drive then!" she gasped. "I can't wait any longer!"

115

Longarm began stroking again, slowly at first, then faster and still faster. Lexie began to writhe almost at once; then after a moment she cried out and began to tremble. Her shudders were short-lived. Her body was soon jerking, her hips twisting, as Longarm continued his quick deep penetrations.

When Lexie's cries grew to a peak and exploded into a single burst of happy bubbles, Longarm drove for a few moments longer before releasing his own control. Then he jetted and held himself pressed hard to Lexie's still-pulsing body until the final wave swept over him and he lay sprawled and still on her now-quiescent body.

Long moments passed before either of them stirred. Longarm moved first. He lifted his head and said, "I ain't really ready to quit, but we better not start again."

"There's nothing I'd like better, you know," she sighed. "But you're right. Just don't wait too long to come back, Longarm. I think we're only beginning to get acquainted."

Riding through the mid-afternoon sunshine and nearing the sheriff's office, Longarm peered ahead and frowned as he gazed up the short slope at its walls.

"Old son," he muttered around the cigar clamped in his teeth, "something just ain't right about that place. That roof wasn't all canted up the way it is now and—"

He broke off and toed his horse to a faster gait. As he reached the narrow trail from the road up the slope to the building his jaw dropped. He was halfway up the slope before he could see the building from an angle that revealed the scattered bricks and the wried bars of the small side window strewn over the ground. The earth was churned into clods where horses' hooves had dug into it, and the next step his horse took enabled him to see the gaping darkness of the diamond-shaped hole in the wall where the high-set barred window had been.

Setting his jaw, an angry frown on his face deepening, Longarm dismounted and started for the ragged-edged opening, but before he'd taken two steps toward it he already knew what he would find inside.

Chapter 10

Wherever he looked on the low slope that led to the broken wall, Longarm saw loose bricks. They were scattered between the half-dozen sets of short deep parallel grooves in the sparsely covered ground, grooves left by the hooves of horses when the animals had strained and dug in while they pulled the window's bars out of the wall. A short length of rope, the woven rope of a lariat, lay among the cracked and broken chunks of bricks. No boot prints showed among the debris, but even if there had been any, Longarm realized that they would be of little or no use to him in tracking the men who'd been responsible for wrecking the jail.

Already certain of what he'd find inside, Longarm crawled through the gap in the wall. His first glance told him that he'd underestimated the damage. More loose bricks were strewn on the floor in the jail area, and the door of the cell where Kelly Sisson had been confined was gaping open. The cell keys on their metal hoop chain dangled from one key that was still in the lock of the cell which the escaped prisoner had occupied, and the door between the cells and the office stood ajar.

Now Longarm could anticipate what he would see when he entered the office, and once more his expectation was fulfilled. The room had been vandalized, the table was overturned, chairs upended. The cot lay on one side, its frame splintered and broken. The desk's drawers were open, papers from them strewn over the floor. In one small area the floor was covered with curled and blackened shards where some of the papers had been burned. Longarm had only to glance around to know what had happened during his absence.

"You made a double-fisted jackass outa yourself, old son," he muttered as he turned his head from side to side, assessing the damage. "Maybe that Lexie was just doing what Sully Briggs told her to, and you got taken in by her. But it don't take more'n one look to tell what went on here. That talk you had with Briggs sure must've rubbed him the wrong way."

While he began digging into the rubbish-strewn floor to find his rifle and saddlebags, Longarm continued to think aloud. "Now Briggs was looking for a killer he could hire, and the closest one handy was that Kelly Sisson, so Briggs sent some of his men to get him outa jail. And Sisson just put in his two cents' worth by trying to set the place on fire. It ain't his fault there wasn't all that much harm done, but now he's free and likely heading for the Scablands, so it's up to you to go after him and get him back."

Even while he was assessing damage and blame, Longarm was deciding on a course of action. With his gear retrieved, he went outside and mounted his horse. At the fork in the road he reined the animal toward the doctor's office.

"I'm sorry as all get-out that I messed things up for you," Longarm concluded after telling Fred Carter what had happened to the jail. "And I aim to make up for it as best I can."

"You'll more than make up for everything if you get this town rid of Sully Briggs," Carter replied. "He's tried to get me on his side more than once, and I've always turned down his offers. What he did up at the jail was hitting out at me as well as you, if you're sure that he's the one behind all this."

"Can you think of anybody else but Briggs who'd be to blame?"

Carter shook his head as he replied, "Oh, it's got Sully's mark, all right. He's out to hogtie this whole town and all the country around it for his own little stamping ground. The way I figure is that he's going to try and push as far as he can while I'm laid up."

"I ain't trying to set myself in your place, or nothing like that," Longarm said. "But I don't figure you're the kind that's going to step to one side and let him have it. Not any more'n I'm going to let Kelly Sisson get away."

"I asked Doc Forbes this morning when he was going to let me out of here," Carter replied. "He said tomorrow morning. I got a hunch he'll say today, after I've told him what's happened."

Longarm shook his head. "Not on your tintype, Fred. You ain't in shape yet for a job like I'm going on. If you was to go with me, I'd hate to take any blame should you get worse."

"I hate to have to agree with you," Carter said. "But I know you're right, Longarm." Regret was reflected in the tone of his voice as he added, "If I was, you and me'd be going together, you after your man and me after mine."

"Sure," Longarm agreed. "But I'll take the will for the deed, Fred."

"Thanks." Carter smiled wryly. "What bothers me is that it's going to take a lot more than willpower to catch Sisson, with Sully Briggs helping him now."

"Two ain't much more trouble than one. I've heard you say that more'n once, Fred."

"And I meant it too." Carter was silent for a moment, then he went on. "Going by yourself into the Scablands won't be any picnic. I can give you a little help here, though. If I push Dr. Forbes a mite, I'm sure he'll let me go out and mind the office. And I can hire some of the men here in town to start cleaning up that mess you've been telling me about."

"It's a mess, all right," Longarm agreed. "Bad as the Scablands. But you ain't going to talk me outa going after 'em and bringing back."

"Just the same, I'd sure like to be on hand, helping you."

"Now, there's one thing you might be able to help me with. You got a map I can take along?"

"I haven't got a map of the Scablands myself. There aren't even any that I know about." Carter frowned. "At least not closer than at the Indian Bureau office, and that'd be a long ride from here."

"Then I'll go without one. Come to think of it, a map wouldn't likely do me much good, from what I seen of the Scablands since I been here," Longarm observed.

"There's not any real good Scablands maps anyhow,"

Carter told Longarm. "Not that it's helping you much to tell you that. But I've found the best way to get around in 'em is to have a compass. Just aim north going and head south coming and when you hit a river follow it upstream or down."

"I use the sun myself," Longarm said. "But there's a compass in my saddlebags, if it ain't got lost. But I just had an idea pop into my head, something that I'd like to get your opinion on."

"Something that'll make the job easier?"

"If it didn't, I wouldn't be talking about it," Longarm told his old friend. "What'd you say if I was to deputize that young blacksmith? If he'd be agreeable to go along with me, he'd likely know the lay of the land and maybe help me slide past a heap of trouble."

"Ben Moore?" Carter asked. Longarm nodded. "I'd say he's as good a man as you'll find in this place. You're right about him knowing the country, and I'd sure feel better if there was somebody like him in the Scablands with you."

"Then I'll stop at his place and see if he cottons to the idea," Longarm said. He stood up and added, "I've already done too much lollygagging, or I'd ride with you back to your office. But the day ain't getting any younger, and I need to be starting right off."

When Longarm reined in at Ben Moore's blacksmith shop, the clink of a hammer on metal told him the young smith was at work. He dropped the reins of his horse and went inside. Moore was holding up a bent and twisted length of strap-iron in his tongs, examining it. He saw Longarm and placed the tongs on the anvil as he turned and nodded a greeting.

"Back so soon, Marshal?" he asked. "Don't tell me

123

there's something wrong with that new shoe I put on your horse."

"Nothing wrong that I could tell, the little bit I've rode him," Longarm replied. "This time I got some other business I want to talk about with you."

"Some part of your gear must need fixing then," Moore said. "Well, I'll do my best to take care of it."

"What business I've got this time's not in your regular line of work," Longarm said. "I don't guess you've heard about what happened out at the sheriff's office?"

"All I know is that some fellow that's got a place down south of town a way said there was something wrong there. He came in this morning, needed a new piece of strap-iron bent for his wagon bed," Moore replied. He gestured toward the wried piece of metal he'd been working on. "He was in a hurry to get back, so I fixed him up as best I could and he started home. I suppose you'd know what happened?"

"A lot better'n I like to," Longarm replied. Then, keeping his explanation as brief as he could, he went on to outline the situation which faced him. "Now, I got to go out in the Scablands and track them fellows," he concluded. "And I got to wondering if you might not be a good man to have along. You know the lay of the land north of here, I guess?"

"I'd say without bragging that I know it about as well as anybody around here," Moore replied.

"Then you've likely heard about a place called Whistling Rock? Because that's where Briggs is likely heading for."

"I guess everybody in these parts has heard about it," the blacksmith said. "And I think I know about where it'd be, but if it's a guide you're thinking about—"

"A guide and maybe a little bit more," Longarm broke in. "I got a hunch about something, and generally when I get one, I've found out it's a pretty good idea to follow it."

"Suppose you tell me exactly what you've got in mind," Moore suggested.

"What'd you say if I asked you to go along? Not just to guide me, though. I ain't had to swear in a special deputy for a good long spell, but when I catch up with Sully Briggs and his crew—and I'm betting he's got one out there besides that killer he got free of the jail—there's likely to be some real trouble."

"Well, Marshal Long, I've put in my hitch with the territorial volunteers," the young blacksmith said. "And I've looked into the wrong end of a redskin's rifle a time or two. I'm not what you'd call a gunfighter, but I'll guarantee to hold up my end if there's trouble. If you need a special deputy, I'd say go ahead and give me whatever kind of swearing-in I need, and I'll ride along with you."

"That's all I could ask of a man," Longarm said. "Now, if you can close up shop a few days, and square things up with your wife—"

Moore interrupted him. "I'm still a single man. And at this time of the year, I'm not going to lose much trade. I live in that little cabin back of the shop, and my rifle's there. It's just an old cut-down Sharps, but it still carries true. My horse is in the corral just past the house. I'm ready to go in the clothes I'm standing up in, so all I'll have to do is close the door and we can set out."

"Then while you get your gear together, I'll ride on up to the closest store and buy what grub we'll be needing," Longarm said. "When I get back, I'll swear you in as a deputy. Then we'll just take off for the Scablands and see if we can't get Kelly Sisson back and give Sully Briggs his comeuppance."

"Once we get across that river up ahead, we'll be able to make better time," Moore told Longarm as he pointed to the scattered glints of dancing brightness that dotted the skyline ahead of them. "The crossing we're headed for is the easiest one hereabouts."

"So you'd be pretty sure that's the way Sully Briggs would've been heading?" Longarm asked.

"It's the way Briggs would've been most likely been making for," the young blacksmith replied. "Anybody that knows the country's going to cross there, where the current's not so fast and the ground's level."

"I guess you've been over a lot of the ground beyond it?"

"Some of it. But away from the river it's pretty much deserted. The going gets rougher too."

"Not much but rocks and sand, like it is along here?"

"Pretty much," Moore answered. "There's homesteaders and squatters all along the rivers and creeks here in the Scablands. Not too many, of course, because most of 'em try to fight shy of Indian land."

"I guess it's mostly Indian land, across the river?"

"Just about all of it used to be," Moore replied. "It was in the Colville Reservation, but settlers—and swindlers like Sully Briggs—keep on nibbling away at the edges."

"I don't know as much as I'd like to about these redskins out here," Longarm went on. "Now, you put me back east in the Indian Nation, and I'd be right at home."

"Well, in the Scablands you'll find Wenatchees and

126

Yakimas and Klickitats and a few Sinkiuses," Moore said. "Not as many as I've heard there used to be. The Cayuses and the Wenatchees and Nez Percé have mostly moved south of the river now, down in the Grand Coulee country."

"How come you know so much about the redskins?" Longarm asked.

"My grandma on my daddy's side was half Nez Percé. She used to tell me Indian stories when I was a tad."

"It sure looks like I picked the right man to deputize." Longarm smiled. "But I don't reckon there's many hostiles left by now, is there?"

"Just a few. There's just one bunch I know of that might give us trouble, that's the Sinkiuses. I've heard that what few's left of them are still pretty mean."

Longarm and Moore talked very little more as they continued moving steadily, letting their horses pick their own way in following the faintly marked path leading to the river. As they rode ahead the ground took on a steeper downward slant. Soon the river came into view. It ran between low banks of barren rock-broken earth, blue-green water roiled with patches of white froth. Longarm spotted the hoofprints first and pointed them out to his companion.

"They're fresh," he said. "Most likely made yesterday, if I ain't mistaken too bad."

"They're the ones we've been looking for, at least I'm pretty sure they are," Moore agreed. "This is the easiest place to cross the Columbia along here, and the land to the west of the big creek that flows into the river a little ways upstream is prime for farming."

"I figured it to be Indian Reservation land, the way it shows on the only map I could find. You mean there's farms and houses on the other side of the river?"

"Not many, because a couple of years before I opened my shop back in Moses there was a big flood here. Some of the houses of folks that'd settled got washed away or tumbled around so much that there wasn't anything but boards left of them."

"And the flood drove a lot of homesteaders away, I guess?" Longarm asked.

"Just about all of them. Mostly those that left just pulled up stakes and moved on. The tough ones put their places back together and started all over again. We'll run across a few up ahead, on the other side of the river."

"It don't look like it's too bad of a crossing," Longarm noted. "From what you've said, I imagine you've made it before?"

"Only a time or two, and not at all lately, not since the big flood three or four years ago." Moore frowned. "There was a spell right after the highest water started going down when all there was along here was mud, almost axle-deep on a wagon wheel and hock-high on a horse's hind legs. That's when folks begun to move out."

"And that'd explain why Sully Briggs picked out this stretch we're heading for and set out to get hold of as much of it as he could lay his hands on," Longarm said. "He figures to sell it on a mortgage and cheat out whoever's bought it any way he can. Then he'll keep it himself, or maybe use it for bait to swindle some other poor devil with."

"But he can't expect to keep on doing business that way," Moore said. "It's not just cheating, Longarm. It's stealing."

"Sure. But he'll keep on doing it, long as nobody calls his hand."

While they talked they'd been advancing steadily toward the river. It flowed only a few yards distant from them now. Both Longarm and Moore had been studying the terrain. A wide expanse of dark mucky soil stretched from their horses' hooves to the white strip of frothy water that ran at the river's edge. The broad expanse of bubbles was opaque. There was no indication of the bottom's nature for as long as they could see in either direction.

Longarm reined in and Moore pulled up beside him. He turned to Longarm and gestured toward the stream as he said, "I don't know whether there'd be any better place close by, either upstream or down. It looks pretty much the same both ways."

"You ain't crossed anyplace else around here?"

"Only at Nespelem Creek. It's about four miles up-river. Just downstream from the creek there's a shoal that lets you splash across. But from the hoofprints we've been following, this is where the ones you're after forded."

"If they did, we can too," Longarm told Moore. "Let's just give it a try. But maybe you better wait here and keep dry till I get across or till I'm so near the other bank that it won't make no never-mind."

As Longarm spoke he was toeing his mount into the water. The horse tossed its head, but splashed into the current. Its hooves slipped a time or two, but it managed to keep moving. Then without warning it began churning with its forefeet as its forequarters plunged downward.

Longarm reacted with the almost instinctive moves he'd acquired during his cowhand days. Leaning back in the saddle, he drew his Colt as he fought the reins with one hand while sliding the revolver between two shirt buttons until he could feel from the chill of the metal that it was safely cradled above his belt and inside his shirt. Then he took his rifle out of its saddle scabbard and held it above his head.

As he held the reins with his freed hand he felt the horse begin swimming. It was nearing a spot only a couple of yards ahead where a large patch of bubbly froth covered the water. An instant or two later the animal reared up, its front hooves churning. Then its hindquarters rose above the water's surface, followed by its belly as its hind feet touched solid bottom once more.

Longarm turned as the horse headed for the shore, now only a dozen or so yards distant. He saw Moore was having the same problem that had faced him. The blacksmith had also grabbed his rifle from its saddle scabbard and was holding it above his head as his horse swam the short distance to the submerged shelf. It reared up just as Longarm's mount had done, and started heading for solid ground.

Longarm lighted a cigar and eased himself in the saddle until he was comfortably relaxed while he waited for his companion to reach his side. As the blacksmith pulled up and reined his dripping mount to a halt, Longarm said, "We made it across, all right. Now how long of a ride are we away from where you figure we might catch up with them scoundrels we're after?"

"It's not going to take us as long as it would've if we'd gone upriver to the other crossing," Moore replied. "But these horses are pretty well tuckered out right now."

"Running into that bad spot in the river sure didn't freshen 'em up none," Longarm agreed.

"We'll need to rest 'em for a little while before we set out again. I'd say that the better part of tomorrow, maybe even the next day, is going to be gone before we can get there."

"Then let's push on without wasting too much time resting," Longarm suggested. "Sully Briggs had to have some reason for taking that damn Kelly Sisson along when he left town."

Moore's voice was thoughtful as he said, "It might've just been that he wanted to get Sisson out of jail before you could take him back east."

"Sure," Longarm agreed. "But it just as well could be that Briggs had a job for him to do out here in the Scablands. Whichever it is, I don't aim to lallygag. The sooner I can put my handcuffs on that killer's wrists, the better I'm going to feel!"

Chapter 11

Since making their river-crossing, Longarm and Ben Moore had been riding steadily, guided only by the declining sun. It was now hanging midway between its zenith and the horizon, almost low enough to begin shining into their faces. The Scablands looked the same in all directions: a seemingly endless expanse of raw light brown earth, rocks, and sparse scrubby vegetation. Where the land slanted its lumpy surface was seamed with cracks and small crevices and gullies.

Here and there the soil was so sparse and thin that rock outcrops were exposed. On level stretches a few touches of green broke the monotony, but Scablands green was not the rich emerald hue of greenery in other places. It was a pale sickly shade. On occasional stretches, in the gullies and shallow hollows, the stems of yellowed weeds rose, quivering now and again when a light hot breeze passed in a brief puff or two before dying away.

"What land I seen while we was getting here was a long way from being bad as this," Longarm told Ben Moore as their horses plodded ahead.

"You're seeing now just about what we'll be traveling through on this side of the big river," the blacksmith replied. "There's an old joke about this part of the territory. When a Scablands man died and stood before the Recording Angel, he was given the choice of going to Hell or going back to his regular life. He told the angel, 'Thanks, but if it's all the same to you, I think I'll just go to Hell. It stands to be a lot better there than where I came from.' "

"I can put up with it for a little while, I guess," Longarm said. "But there's a lot of other places I'd sooner be, if I had my druthers."

Though Longarm and Moore had not pressed their horses, the animals were beginning to move more and more slowly. The riders had no idea how far they'd traveled, for judging distances was next to impossible without fixed landmarks for reference. Longarm's horse had pulled ahead of his companion's on the long curving upslope they'd just mounted after crossing a barren saucerlike valley. When he finally got to the rim of the long haul Longarm reined in. Ben Moore pulled up his horse when he reached Longarm.

"For all the time we're making now, it'll be tomorrow or next day before we get to where we're heading," Longarm remarked. He'd looped his reins around the saddlehorn, fished a cigar out of his pocket, and he took out a match and scratched his thumbnail across it. The match flamed and Longarm puffed his cigar alight before going on. "You got any idea how much further it is?"

134

"I haven't seen any landmarks I've recognized since we started out from last night's camp," Moore replied. "But like I told you back in town, it's been a good long spell since I've had a job away from town that's brought me up to this stretch of country."

"Even if you ain't been here lately, you're bound to remember something about it."

"I recall the way the land looks, even if I've only ridden over it a few times," Moore assured him. "And I remember somebody back in town mentioning something about a pretty fair-sized lake someplace around here. It's called Ocamache or maybe it was Omache. Whichever they call it, the lake's somewheres hereabouts, but I never have seen it in the few times I've come into this part of the country."

"You're sure you don't have any idea how close the lake might be?" Longarm asked. "Generally, I ain't one to push a man like I'm doing you, but we'll be needing fresh water, for us and the horses too. I don't have a bit of hankering to drink the muddy slop in them puddles that's all we've seen since we crossed that river."

Moore shook his head, then he said, "The trouble is that I never have seen the lake. I've got a feeling that I ought to remember this part of the Scablands, but I've always come in from the south instead of the way we've circled trying to keep on what little trail Briggs and Sisson might've left."

"That'd make a lot of difference, I got to agree," Longarm said through the smoke of his cigar. "A course, it's all strange country to me. The only thing I know to name in it is that Whistling Rock place you've told me about. I don't reckon it'd have a name like that if it didn't make some kinda noise to match it."

"It whistles, all right, when there's even a little bit of wind blowing. And I'd know Whistling Rock if I saw it again, just like you would if you saw it. Pretty close by it, there's a little creek that flows into a sink." Moore paused. "There's not much way we can miss it, because it's a tall skinny rock that sticks up like a finger with a big wad of chewing tobacco on top of it. It sure seems a lot further than I remember it, though."

"I guess about all we can do is ride along and keep on looking," Longarm said. "If we prowl around enough, we'll turn up Briggs sooner or later."

"Sure," the blacksmith agreed. "We've spotted enough hoofprints and fresh horse-dung to know they passed along here. And if we once catch sight of that Whistling Rock, we can guide by it to where Sully Briggs's settlement is."

"It's likely," Longarm agreed. "So let's you and me just push on and keep close watch on the sky. Sully Briggs and whoever's with him'll be needing a cook-fire. We'd see its smoke a long ways off as long as daylight holds out."

"That'd put us right onto them," Moore said. "Except that dark's going to catch up with us, and if we can't tell too much about where we're heading in daylight, we're likely to get really mixed up after night sets in."

"We still got a pretty good spell of daylight left," Longarm said. "And even if we get caught by the dark I can guide us some by the stars. But that ain't going to help much when we don't know perzactly where we need to be heading."

"You figure to keep traveling after it gets dark then?"

"Not unless we see some sorta light up ahead. Even with the moon full like it is now, a fire's going to reflect off the sky after sunset's over. Let's us get a move on before that sky-glow turns red and it starts to get plumb dark."

They were starting up from the bottom of a long incline now. It was steeper than most of the rising ground, and their tiring horses began to breathe hard. Longarm could feel the barrel of his mount expanding and contracting, the broken rhythm of its breathing warning him that the animal was getting badly winded. Though there was still a long stretch of rising ground ahead, he reined in.

"You go on and push ahead," Longarm told Moore. "I got to favor this nag and stop for a little bit. If you see anything worth looking at, or the ground levels out up ahead, you might wait on the top of the rise for me to catch up with you."

Moore nodded and toed his horse's flank with his boot toe. The tiring animal responded, its hooves sending up little spurts of gravel and dust as it fought its way up the grade. After Longarm had reined in he shifted to sit sideways in his saddle. He took out a cigar and lighted it, still keeping his eyes on his companion.

When Moore reached the crest of the rise he turned in his saddle to wave to Longarm. While he continued waving with one hand he began to point with his other at something that was hidden from Longarm's eyes by the broken crestline. Moore held his position for a moment, then disappeared over a high shoulder that rose on the crest of the upslope.

Longarm continued to watch the ragged line of rising rocky ground where Moore had disappeared, looking for him to emerge beyond the humped shoulder that broke the jagged rim. When several moments passed and Moore did not reappear, a frown formed on Longarm's face. He waited for another moment or two, then prodded his horse's flank with his boot toe and started toward the crest of the rise.

Even before he'd reached the top Longarm saw the outline of a strange object coming into view above the rim of the slope. It was not part of the rim, but stood some distance away from it. He continued his slow advance, losing some ground now and then when the treacherous loose rock under his horse's hooves gave way to a small rockslide that set the horse to scrambling its hooves on the uncertain footing as it fought to keep its balance.

Bobbing back and forth in his saddle, Longarm managed to hold himself in the saddle of the scrambling swaying animal. As he got within a few yards from the crest of the slope he began to see more clearly that what had attracted his attention was an almost unbelievably high pillar of rock rising near the center of the small mountain's almost circular interior valley. The towering formation was topped by a bulging flattened boulder that seemed to defy all of nature's laws by balancing on the very apex of the rock column.

Before he'd quite reached the narrow curving top of the small mountain, a strange soughing whine struck Longarm's ears. It was not loud, but the waves of fluttering sound were pitched so high that they almost masked the noise that was being made by his mount's scrabbling hooves. He was pulling at the reins to stop his horse when realization struck him.

"Damned if that ain't got to be Whistling Rock, old son!" he exclaimed. Before Longarm had finished speaking his voice was echoing loudly in his ears, for the weird noise stopped as unexpectedly as it had begun.

With the return of silence Longarm's interest in the column of stone ended as suddenly as the noise itself. He looked around and saw that he was still a few yards from the end of the grade. He nudged the horse again with his boot toe to send the animal the remaining distance to the rim of the slope.

Ahead of him the rim stretched broad and barren, unlike the broken, cracked, and stone-strewn surface of the ground below. It bore the rounded pocks of hoofprints and an occasional old and weather-beaten scattered dung pile, and Longarm's eyes opened a bit wider when among the prints he saw the even more subtle oval impressions of moccasined feet. Even among the maze of other marks, Longarm could identify the hoofprints of Ben Moore's horse, for they were imprinted on top of other footprints and hoofprints in all the areas of soft drifted earth.

Longarm studied the path for a moment, then returned his attention to the rock pillar and the massive boulder on its tip. After he'd studied them for several moments and could reach no conclusion as to their significance, the lack of an explanation led him further. He touched the horse's flank with his boot heel and reined the animal ahead.

With Longarm keeping the reins loose enough to signal the horse that it was to keep moving steadily, he was free to study the ground ahead of him. The prints of Ben Moore's horse were still imprinted on the trail over a mixture of other hoofprints and the marks of human footprints. These were not the sharply outlined prints of men wearing boots, but the full-foot impression of moccasins.

"Old son," Longarm told himself as he advanced, speaking a little below a whisper, "them's redskin sign, and real fresh too. From the way it looks, Ben wasn't watching his p's and q's and them rascals took him by surprise. There ain't no sign him or anybody else got hurt, so someplace right up ahead them rascals have got him, sure as God made little green apples. And there ain't nobody but you around to get him free of 'em."

Pulling his rifle from its slanting scabbard, Longarm rested the Winchester across the pommel of his saddle and continued his slow, steady approach. The trail that he was following kept its downward spiral around the face of the mountain, describing a sharp inward curve when the contour of the rise dictated it, and bending inward or sharply outward as the terrain demanded.

A glance ahead showed Longarm that he'd almost reached the cliff's base. There, the trail jogged sharply around one of the riblike formations that bulged from the side of the towering cliff. The reins in his hand kept slipping and he loosened his grip on them to move his hand closer to the horse's shoulders, holding his rifle away from his side as he started to bend forward in the saddle.

Longarm began to change his grip on the reins. They were slack in his right hand and in his left he gripped his rifle. Before he could lift the weapon's butt from its resting place on his thigh, its muzzle pointing to the sky, he felt the cold steel of another rifle's muzzle jam into the back of his neck.

As the chill of the rifle muzzle met Longarm's flesh a harsh voice commanded, "Drop rifle, white devil! I shoot if you not do!"

In that moment Longarm knew that he'd lost the first round, but he promised himself silently that there would be others which he would win. He did not try to move his head, but opened his hand and let his rifle drop to the ground. As yet he'd not gotten a glimpse of the man who'd taken him by surprise, and he made no effort to turn his head and look even after a shrill whistle from his captor almost deafened him as it pierced the air close by.

Longarm remained motionless when a pattering of moccasined feet sounded beyond the curve in the trail and a half-dozen breechclout-clad Indians came running to surround his horse. One of them scooped up Longarm's rifle, another pulled his Colt from its holster. Then they backed away from him a half step and stopped. One stood on either side of his horse, holding Longarm's ankles to keep him from removing his feet from the stirrups or from kicking the horse into a sudden burst of movement.

Being careful not to move his head, Longarm flicked his eyes from one of his captors to another. He was surprised at their youth, for he saw not a single wrinkled face among the four who were within the restricted range of his vision. Those he could see without turning his head or moving had no war-paint. They only wore breech-clouts. All of them had sheath-knives tucked into the narrow woven leather belts that supported the breechclouts, which were decorated with long leather thongs dangling to mid-thigh, but the knives seemed to be the extent of their weaponry.

"Get off your horse now," the man next to him said. "And do not move foolishly."

To Longarm's surprise, the Indian's voice was quite level and his speech was not gutturally intoned, as was that of most of the Indians he'd encountered on the plains. He'd taken Longarm's rifle from the Indian who'd retrieved it, but he did not raise it to threaten Longarm.

"We have already captured the other man," the Indian went on. "He will not be able to help you."

"Neither me nor him came here to make trouble for you," Longarm said as he swung out of his saddle and turned to face the Indian. "I'm a deputy United States marshal, and we ain't interested in what you and your men are doing, or why you ain't on your reservation where you oughta be. We're looking for some outlaws that're from way to the south of here."

Longarm paused for breath, his eyes fixed on the Indian in front of him. When the man made no reply, he went on. "Now, you talk like a man that's had good schooling, so you oughta know the best thing you can do is be reasonable. Just let us go on about our business, and we won't bother you a bit when you go about yours."

For a long moment the Indian did not reply. He stood studying Longarm, while the others of his group stood in stony-faced silence. Just as the man was opening his mouth to reply, the eerie wail of Whispering Rock broke the air for a second time with its strange harshly doleful penetrating dissonance. The rising and falling intonation lasted longer than it had a few minutes earlier, and ended as abruptly as it had begun.

At last the Indian broke his silence. "We not kill you now," he said. His voice was thin and flat, without expression. "But we will not let you go. Come, we will take you to our camp. It is not far from here."

Longarm had played enough poker to know the value of an expressionless face and a silent bluff. He did not change his expression and said nothing as the Indian turned to the men holding him and barked a few harsh commands. One of the men holding him drew his sheath-knife and cut off one of the long knee-length leather strips that dangled from his belt.

142

When the Indian stepped up to him and pulled his arms down, Longarm did not resist. He had no intention of wasting his strength struggling, and kept his arms loose when the man pulled them behind his back and bound his wrists together with the thong he'd cut from his belt. The Indian moved swiftly and surely as he carried out the leader's orders, and when Longarm flexed his muscles to test the bonds they did not yield.

A quick volley of commands from the leader set the group into motion. Two of the younger Indians took charge of Longarm's horse and started leading it along the faint trail that zigzagged down the slope. No more commands were given by the leader. He simply gripped Longarm's biceps and tugged, then gestured for the remainder of the group to close in around them. As they moved to obey the leader motioned toward the faint downhill trail and started walking.

As he'd done earlier, Longarm let the man lead him. As they started down the narrow winding trail the remainder of the little group formed into a close crowd around Longarm and their commander. The path slanted sharply downhill. Its surface was rough and littered with loose rocks, but from the actions of the Indians Longarm judged that they were in no hurry.

Longarm's walk ended much more quickly than he'd expected. They'd been moving for only a short time when the men at the front of the little procession seemed suddenly to vanish. Longarm discovered the reason when the chief tugged at his bonds to turn him sidewise and half-led, half-pulled him into a narrow cleft that zig-zagged through the face of the bluff.

Here the going was a bit more difficult, for the fissure was not only dark, it was not quite wide enough to allow them to walk abreast. With a large measure of pushing by the Indians behind them and a bit of body-twisting and sidling on the part of Longarm and the leader, they moved along the fissure's narrow, sharply slanting floor between the high ragged stone walls that soon rose far above their heads on both sides.

What Longarm had expected to be a long passage into a cavern was instead a relatively short one through a cleft. There was never a moment when the slit of darkening sky overhead was blocked. Then the cleft widened suddenly and Longarm looked across a roughly circular valley. Its floor was broken only by the high monolithic column that rose near its center.

Though Longarm knew quite well that the towering pillar topped by the unusual rock formation was the same one he'd gotten a glimpse of from the valley's rim, it now presented an entirely different aspect. His brief look from above had given no hint of the height of the supporting column, which now showed its true mass and altitude.

Longarm's earlier view of it from above had emphasized its size rather than its mushroomlike form. Now the capping boulder seemed to be only an extension of its supporting stone formation. While Longarm was still gazing at the column the Indian whose captive he'd been as they passed through the slit in the canyon wall tugged at the bonds that secured his wrists.

"Come!" he commanded. "We have much to do before the dark comes down."

Well aware of his situation, Longarm moved ahead. The Indian led him on into the circular valley. Its floor was not quite as barren as most of the terrain which Longarm and Ben Moore had crossed, but it had no vegetation other than shortgrass and here and there a clump of weeds. Ahead of them, a blocky building took shape. Concealing his surprise, Longarm studied it. Crowded as it was against the high stone wall the building looked small and seemed to be only a bulge in the towering formation to which it appeared attached.

Longarm's captor stopped when they reached the building and gestured toward a door. A younger Indian was hunkered down beside it, a rifle across his thighs. Longarm recognized the weapon as Ben Moore's cut-down Sharps, but before he could begin wondering what had happened to his companion, the two Indians exchanged a few words in a language which he was unable to understand. Then the man who'd been on guard duty opened the door and Longarm's escort shoved him inside. The door slammed closed.

As Longarm stood blinking in the darkness of the strange room Ben Moore's familiar voice broke the silence.

"Longarm!" Moore exclaimed. "So they caught up with you too! I was hoping you'd show up, but I figured you'd come in shooting and maybe give us both a chance to get away. Now we've got to get our heads together quick, because these damn redskins have got it all figured out to kill us!"

Chapter 12

"I ain't a bit surprised to hear you say that," Longarm said to Moore. "But tell me how come you know such a lot about what they aim to do."

"I heard them talking about it when they were bringing me here. They were—"

"Hold on a minute," Longarm said. A frown had formed on his face as he spoke. "Did I understand you right? You did say you heard 'em talking, didn't you?"

"Yes, of course," Moore replied, a bit of impatience tingeing his voice. "Why shouldn't I have heard 'em? My ears are as good as the next man's."

"Hearing and understanding ain't quite the same," Longarm went on. "You said something before about blacksmithing on the big reservation over east in the Scablands for a spell, but I don't recall you mentioning that you learned any Indian lingo."

"Well, there wasn't any need to. But I picked up a

word or two here and there. It's mostly pidgin, and I guess I sound to them just like they do to me. But when you come down to it, there's not much difference between Okanogan and Spokane and Yakima and Sinkiuse and all the others. Anyhow, these redskins were talking pretty good English."

"I guess that'd follow," Longarm said. "They'd've had time to learn it, if they was on the reservation very long. But go ahead, I didn't mean to bust in on what you was about to say."

"It wasn't much, because they don't talk a lot. But they were figuring out a way to capture you too."

"Which they done, the more fool me," Longarm said. "But that don't make no never-mind. I ain't going to let no redskin brags upset me and get my mind off of our main worry, which is for us to get outa here before they get a chance to do anything about killing either one of us."

"I'll sure put in with you on that," Moore said. "But I'd like to know how we can get away, not without guns or horses or much else to help us."

"Well, now," Longarm said, "we'll just have to do some quick figuring. So far, it looks like to me like we been about even-Steven with luck until we sorta played the fool. If we'd watched our p's and q's we wouldn't be in a fix like we are now."

"We could be in a worse one, I guess," Moore said wryly. "For one thing, both of us could be dead and scalped by now."

"I ain't going to argufy over that," Longarm told him. "It's a nine-day wonder they didn't just get rid of us."

He spoke absentmindedly, for he was blinking rapidly to get his eyes accustomed to the gloom. All that he could see at the moment was Moore's figure a step or two away from him, a vague outline in the darkness.

"Right now, I feel pretty lucky too," the blacksmith said after a moment's silence.

"Meaning what? That you're still alive?"

"Not just that, Longarm, even if they could've killed me right off if they'd had a notion to," Moore replied. "This might sound funny, locked up the way we are, but with both of us here, I feel like we've got a chance to break free now."

"That's one way to look at it, I reckon. And I'd sure liefer be free than locked up. How'd they manage to take you?"

"I just wasn't watching close enough, I guess," Moore told him. "All I know is, I went around one of those curves in the trail, maybe a half mile or more past the place I left you. The first time I had a hint there was an Indian—or anybody else except you—within a hundred miles was when they jumped me."

"How many of 'em was there?"

"Four or five in the bunch that grabbed me. Then there were three more that I got a glimpse of before they brought me to this place and locked me up. I imagine there's a good chance of me not seeing some of them, so maybe there's more."

Longarm nodded and said, "I counted seven in the bunch that got me. All of 'em was young bucks except the one that I taken to be the chief. If I ain't forgot how to cipher, that'd mean there's about fifteen."

"Don't you think it's safe to figure that there might be some Indians around that neither one of us saw?"

"I'd say it's likely. But it don't make much never-mind right this minute," Longarm pointed out. "A course, it

149

will when we start working to get out."

"You sound awfully sure we'll be able to get out."

"Oh, we'll manage. I reckon we was both a mite careless, but I didn't think there was any hostiles left running free in these parts."

"There's not supposed to be," Moore said. "I'm sure about one thing, though. They're reservation-jumpers."

"They're bound to be," Longarm agreed. "From what you seen of 'em, did you get any idea about what tribe they might be from?"

Moore frowned, shook his head. "I've only been on the Colville Reservation—oh, maybe once or twice since I set up my shop in Moses three years ago. I haven't been there at all lately. But like I told you, I do know there's Indians on it from a whole lot of tribes that used to claim this part of the Territory. Why? Does it make any difference what tribe they're from?"

"It just might. When you run into redskins I've found that some's real mean fighters and some'll turn out to be the peaceful kind. Except I've found there's generally more of the mean ones than there is them that's peaceful."

"That stands to reason," Moore agreed. "But what bothers me mostly is that there's only two of us, and we already know there's a lot more of them."

"You don't have to keep reminding me. I played the fool, letting 'em grab me, and I got to admit I wasn't minding where I was the way I oughta been. But that don't make no never-mind now. The milk's been spilt and we've already stepped into it. What we got to do now is figure a way that'll get us out and let our feet get dry."

"Without our guns? And with such a big bunch of them to handle?"

150

"Oh, they got my Winchester and my holster Colt," Longarm replied. "But they wasn't real careful when they searched me. They didn't tumble to the little side-load Colt derringer I got tucked away in back of my belt buckle."

"Well, I'll be damned!" Moore exclaimed. "It never entered my mind that a lawman like you might be carrying one of those whore's guns, Longarm."

"Them redskins didn't think about it either," Longarm went on. "And I don't let on to many folks that I've got it handy. It's a right good little stash-gun, though. Throws a .41 slug that'll knock a man down. A course, its a side-loader, and I only got two quick shots, then I got to reload. I'd a sight rather have six rounds, but we ain't going to need only maybe two or three shots, if we work it right."

"Just what do you mean by working it right?"

"It looks to me like there's two things we can do." Longarm's voice was soberly thoughtful. "One is we can try to bust out right now, while there's enough light for us to see what's what and which way we're going. The other one is that we can wait till it gets dark and take our chances."

"Which one do you like best?"

"What I like best and what'd be best don't always jibe," Longarm answered. "Now, we got maybe two or three hours of daylight left. But what I figure is this. Redskins ain't much for fighting at night, so maybe we better wait and be ready to make our try after it's plumb dark."

"How do you think we should do it?" Moore asked.

"Here's how I figure it," Longarm replied. "If we're going to have a chance to break free and clear, we'll need our guns and our horses."

151

"Not finding fault, Longarm," Moore said. "But I'd like to know how we're going to do that, with just that little popgun of yours the only weapon between us."

"I ain't got around to figuring that out yet," Longarm admitted. "Anymore'n I've figured out how we're going to get the door to this black hole opened up. I got a little bit more thinking to do, but I'm trying to work it out. We ain't been in here all that long, and it's still a good while before dark, so maybe we can puzzle out something."

"Say we do come up with a way to get out. After dark in a place where we don't know our way around ain't the best time to be moving around."

"Oh, I'll grant you that," Longarm agreed. "But redskins' eyes and ears ain't any better'n ours."

"If they've got any sense there'll be a guard standing all night outside the door to this place," Moore pointed out. "It's a pretty safe bet he'll have a gun of some kind."

"Don't be too sure," Longarm said. "Think back a minute. Did you see ary a gun but the one that fellow guarding the door to this place was holding?"

"Come to think of it, I didn't," Moore agreed. "But now they've got your rifle and mine and your sixgun too."

"Having a gun and knowing how to use it is two different things," Longarm pointed out. "And from the way they handled them guns of ours, they don't know more about using 'em than I'd know how to diaper a newborn baby."

"So all we've got to do is break down the door without the guard hearing us, and take his gun if he's got one, and then get away without rousing the rest of the bunch."

"That's about the size of it," Longarm said. "But it might not be as bad as looks first on. This here build-

152

ing—or at least that front wall—is 'dobe, and you can bust a hole in it with a boot heel, except it'd take too long to make one big enough for both of us to worm out of. There ain't a window, so the door's the only way I see to get out. And we'd have to be right spry about busting it down."

"I'll agree with that," Moore said. "But I suppose we can do it if we have to."

"Oh, sure. Though if I had my druthers, I'd try to get out right now, soon as we got a chance to. We can—"

Longarm broke off when a rasping of metal against metal sounded from the doorway. He gestured for Moore to stand on one side of the door and took his place on the opposite side. The door swung open, and what seemed in the gloom to be an uncountable number of Indians flooded in, pushing and shoving one another as they fanned out into the shadowed room.

Moore was on the hinged side of the door and when it opened the door itself hid him for a moment. Longarm became the first target of the inrushing Indians. He had not had time to draw his derringer from its hidden place behind his belt buckle, and had no chance to do so now.

Three of the Indians grabbed Longarm and lifted him off the floor before he could take a step back and gain the time needed to move his hand to his belt and get out the little derringer. Even if Longarm had been able to reach it and bring down one or two of them, there would have been more than enough remaining to seize him and immobilize him before he could work the clumsy side-loading derringer's mechanism and slide fresh shells into its barrels.

Longarm tried to writhe free of the Indians' gripping hands, but there were too many of them holding him. By

153

this time the Indians had discovered Moore in his futile hiding place behind the door. He was also losing the battle to break away. Moore was kicking strenuously, but uselessly. Within a few moments he had also been lifted off the floor, the Indians holding his feet and hands.

For a moment the entire group in the shadowed cabin froze, forming a tableau that might have been posed by a group of actors on a stage who were waiting for a photographer to trip the shutter of his camera. Then the motionless moment passed and one of the Indians barked a guttural command. The men who were holding Longarm and Moore pushed their captives facedown on the floor, where they were pinned facedown by the pressure of Indian feet on their backs. Then, with strips of leather from the fringes that decorated their breechclouts, Indians began binding the two captives.

Their work was fast but thorough. When they'd finished their jobs neither Longarm nor the blacksmith could move except to turn their heads and wriggle their fingers. A moment later, when they were lifted to their feet, they also found that their ankles and knees were bound so tightly that they could not stand without toppling over unless one of the Indians held them erect.

"What do you suppose—" Moore began, but stopped short when Longarm frowned and shook his head.

Ben Moore's unfinished question was answered silently by the action of the Indians. Two of the largest stepped up. One picked up Longarm, the other Moore. Tossing the captives over their shoulders like meal sacks, the Indians started for the door.

In spite of their uncomfortable situation, Moore twisted his head until he could see Longarm's face and raised his eyebrows in a silent question. Longarm could

154

answer only with an almost imperceptible shrug. By the time their signals had been exchanged the Indians carrying the helpless captives had reached the door.

As they emerged into daylight after the almost total darkness of the room in which they'd been confined, the glow of sunshine was painful. The eyes of both Longarm and Moore began watering, and their vision was clouded for several moments. They blinked, trying to get rid of the shimmering tears.

When they could see clearly again it was instantly obvious to both captives that the day was drawing closer to its end. The sun had lost much of its brilliant yellow glow. It hung in a cloudless sky, the bottom of the disc only a short distance above the jagged rim of the craterlike valley, the odd formation atop Whistling Rock silhouetted against its dazzling light. The shadows cast by the little procession showed on the valley's floor in long exaggerated moving streaks of black.

Then Longarm discovered that by twisting his head while lifting it as high as possible he could see a surprisingly large area of both the valley and the sky. Only the base of the towering formation which supported Whistling Rock broke his view of the vista. After a quick glance disclosed nothing that was either helpful or interesting, Longarm abandoned the back-straining position he'd twisted himself into and simply hung inert and unmoving across the shoulder of the man who was carrying him.

Ahead of him, Longarm saw that Moore was also being carried in the same fashion that he found so uncomfortable, and that the Indians were moving parallel to the valley's wall. Craning his neck to look back, Longarm saw that a rearguard of three or four Indians was following them.

Their trip along the valley wall was mercifully short, a matter of a hundred yards or less. Longarm found himself dumped off the Indian's shoulder. He landed with a thud on the hard ground. A few yards away he saw that Moore was also falling.

Twisting his head as best he could while lying face-down in a position that cramped him uncomfortably, Longarm peered toward the valley's wall, only a dozen or so yards away. Two small leafless trees stood between them and the wall's abrupt rise. A few paces from where he and Moore were lying he saw more Indians. They were moving around constantly, and Longarm had trouble counting them, but he finally arrived at a tally of fourteen or fifteen.

He saw at his first glimpse that there were no women among them, for the Indians wore only breechclouts. Their torsos were smeared with greasy-looking red and yellow paint, their faces striped with red, and their ebony-black hair fell loose behind their shoulders. They had no weapons that he could see other than sheath-knives stuck in the narrow leather strips that supported the fringes of their thigh-length hide skirts.

Keeping his voice low, Longarm asked Moore, "You got any idea what tribe them redskins belong to?"

"Not the faintest notion," the blacksmith replied. "But I don't have any Indian customers back in Moses. And I don't recall seeing any that looked like this bunch while I was working on the reservation."

"It looks like what you heard them saying about them killing us was right," Longarm went on. "But I sure don't aim to let 'em go ahead."

"How do you figure you can stop them?"

"I'm still trying to figure that out. It's bound to come to me, sooner or later."

As the Indians drew closer, Longarm could see that most of them were young bucks, entering their prime of life. One of them was the man who'd been on guard at the door of the room where he and Moore had been held prisoner. He carried a long deerskin-swathed bundle. Now he laid it on the ground. Longarm set his jaw and tightened his lips to keep from exclaiming when the man opened the bundle and revealed his Winchester as well as Moore's Sharps and a third rifle, a long muzzle-loader even older and larger than the Sharps. It was of such ancient vintage that Longarm hardly recognized it as a rifle.

"If you've got any ideas about how to stop all this, it's time to trot them out," Moore whispered. "Because I sure don't have any."

"I'm in about the same fix you are," Longarm replied. "But let's hold on a minute or two longer. I sure don't like this one little bit."

"No more do I," Moore agreed.

"Well, it looks like something's going to happen pretty soon," Longarm said as he jerked his head toward the Indians. "But that ain't to say we got to like it."

The Indians were moving now, led by a man walking a pace or so in advance of the group. He was older than those following him, and his hair revealed his age. It was almost totally white. Then as the little band drew closer and halted a few paces away, Longarm saw that the leader's face was seamed with a maze of deep wrinkles and the skin of his chest and arms and legs hung loose, as though it had little solid flesh or muscle underlying it.

"Now we can see 'em plainer, you got any idea what tribe that bunch might come from?" Longarm kept his voice to an almost inaudible whisper as he asked the question.

"I know they don't look like Yakimas or Wenatchees, but outside of that I haven't got a notion," the blacksmith replied. "And I don't see what that's got to do with anything that'd help us right now."

"I guess it don't, but—" Longarm stopped short as the aged Indian turned to the group following him and began to speak. To his surprise, the man spoke in pidgin English. Then Longarm realized belatedly that the oldster's tribe must have declined during the intertribal fighting of earlier years, and with the decline his native language had been lost by lack of use.

"Do not kill," the old man said. He raised his hand and placed it on his chest over his heart as he shook his head. Raising the hand to his head he said, "Do not aim here. Not here, kill fast." Then, bending somewhat shakily to move his hand to his thighs and legs, he went on. "Here first, no walk, no run." He rubbed his lower abdomen and said, "Here, kill slow."

Each time the ancient Indian spoke, the younger men around him had nodded their understanding. Longarm and Moore had been able to do nothing more than exchange covert glances during the old Indian's exposition. As the Indian went on both captives realized the significance of his words and gestures.

Moore's eyes widened as the lesson progressed and the old man began giving the younger ones instructions in handling the rifles. He turned to look at Longarm, whose features remained as fixed and inscrutable as he'd learned to keep them during a high-stakes poker game. Longarm shook his head before Moore could speak, and pressed his lips into an almost invisible line to signal the need to remain silent. While they were exchanging looks the old Indian turned away from the young men and stepped up to Longarm and Moore.

When they saw him at little more than arm's length, the leader looked even more ancient than he had at a distance. His obsidian eyes were half-veiled by loose lids that were crimped by tiny overlapping wrinkles, but they glinted with a triumphal shine as he flicked them between Longarm and Moore during the moments that passed while he examined them closely. At last he nodded, then he spoke for the first time.

"I am Kadihan," he announced. His voice was thin and cracked, but his English now was fluent and almost totally unaccented. He waited for a moment before going on. "I am the last of the real Sinkiuse, but the young men you see there will be Sinkiuse soon. I tell you this so that before you die you can make a medicine prayer to your gods and ask them to take you to them."

Chapter 13

"Hold on!" Longarm said quickly. "You got no reason to kill us, if that's what you're figuring to do! Neither me nor him has ever hurt you nor none of your men!"

"This thing may be true," Kadihan replied. "But it is of no matter. All white-skins are our enemies. Can you say you have never killed one of our people?"

Longarm was silent for a moment, then he said, "I ain't saying yes and I ain't saying no. If I did, there wasn't any of 'em from your tribe. And I didn't kill 'em because of what color their skins was. My job's to see the law's kept, and a lawbreaker looks all the same to me whether his skin's white or brown or black or green."

"What you are telling me is that you have a duty," Kadihan said. "But you are not the only man who has. I have one, for I am Sinkiuse. It is my duty to kill whoever kills my people. This is what your people have done. They killed so many that now Matiso, my only son, and

161

I are the last fighting men of our tribe."

"You can't blame that on me and my friend," Longarm said quickly. "What you're talking about happened a long time back."

"That is not important," the old Indian said. "What I think of is that I have a work I cannot stop. It is to keep my tribe living."

"We sure ain't getting in your way if that's what you're trying to do," Longarm explained. "And I don't see no reason why your men jumped us."

"You do not understand," Kadihan replied. "Before a young man can become a fighting man of the Sinkiuse, he must kill one of the fighting men from an enemy tribe."

"Well, that don't take in either one of us," Longarm said. "Because even if you might not think so, we ain't got nothing against you or your people. We're lawmen, and right now we're out after some white rascals that're killers and robbers. We don't have no grudges with you."

Kadihan shrugged as he went on. "Your people have fought my people and my people have fought yours since the first time they came together. I must keep my tribe alive so we can keep fighting."

"You know you ain't going to win," Moore said.

"This may be true," Kadihan answered. "It will not stop me. I have taught these young men all the things I know, except one. I have taught them how to use weapons, but they have not yet killed."

Longarm was silent for a moment, not quite believing what he'd heard. Playing for time now, he said, "Well, it looks to me like there's plenty of wild critters you can watch 'em hunt down, out here in the Scablands."

"We have had too little power for them to shoot my

162

son's gun," the old man told Longarm. "And it is old. It is not the kind they must learn to use. They must shoot with new guns such as yours. And it is not little animals they must learn to kill, but you with white skins. You are our enemies!"

"Hold on, now!" Longarm exclaimed. "That just ain't so. And I don't mean to call you a liar, but if us white men was as bad as you make us out to be, we'd've wiped out you redskins a long time ago!"

"That is what you did!" Kadihan shouted. "White men have killed all my tribe, and that is why you must die! My young fighting men will kill you! We will begin it now."

Longarm could not quite believe what he'd heard. He glanced quickly at Moore. The young blacksmith was staring, his jaw hanging down, his mouth open wide, surprise flooding his face. At last Longarm found his voice.

"Wait a minute!" he protested. "Fighting and killing ain't the same thing! What'd be a real test for them men of yours is to fight us when we can fight back at 'em! That's what you oughta be after!"

As though he had not heard, Kadihan turned to the young Indians and gestured toward Longarm and Moore as he said, "Here are your enemies."

A subdued murmur of anticipation rippled through the group of young men around him. Then one of them asked, "How are so many of us going to kill so few of them?"

"You will each shoot one time," Kadihan replied. "Do not kill them quickly. Aim not for their heart or head. Shoot them in the places I have shown you."

Again the young men crowded around the old chief

163

murmured to one another. Then one of them asked, "Which of us will get the honor of shooting first?"

"We have three guns," Kadihan told him. "Divide into three war parties, as you must learn to do when you attack. One of you in each party will shoot, then pass the gun to another. Matiso and I will show you what you must do to put new shells in. You must remember to aim as I have told you, for these men must not die too soon. When they do, each of you will have shared in killing an enemy. Then you will be Sinkiuse warriors."

A subdued murmur of under-the-breath chattering whispers ran through the young Indians. Then one of them stepped up to Kadihan and asked, "Are we to shoot them where they are now?"

Kadihan shook his head. He pointed to the pair of leafless trees standing a few feet away from the valley wall and said, "Tie them there." He gestured to a small rise in the ground a few paces distant. "At that place you will stand to shoot." Waving to the three rifles lying on the blanket a few paces distant he said, "There are the guns. All of you have fired Matiso's. He will show you how to use the others. Now, tie the white devils to the trees and we will begin."

Longarm and Moore had no chance to improve their situation while Kadihan's small army picked them up and carried them to the trees. The Indians propped Longarm against one tree, Moore against the other, and lashed them to the trunks. Kadihan waved the Indians toward the place where Matiso was waiting with the rifles. They turned and started back at a quick trot.

"These lashings ain't too tight," Longarm observed as the Indians trotted away.

"If we try to break loose, they'll just shoot us on the

164

run," Moore said. "But that don't need to keep us from trying."

Watching as Kadihan led the young Indians to the blanket where the three rifles were lying, both men began straining against their bonds. They saw Matiso rise to his feet as Kadihan and the young Indians reached the blanket where the guns lay.

"We better hurry up," Longarm said. His voice was taut, but otherwise expressionless. "It won't be no time at all till they'll start spitting lead at us."

"I'm doing all I can," Moore told him. "You feel any give in your lashings? Because I sure don't in mine."

"Maybe a little bit. Not much."

Longarm's voice was abstracted. He was watching the progress the Indians were making. The young men had now reached the blanket where the guns lay and were clustered around it. Matiso leaned forward to pick up the old oversized muzzle-loader and handed it to one of the young Indians chosen by Kadihan to be a Sinkiuse warrior. When the boy handled the weapon clumsily and barely avoided dropping it, both Kadihan and Matiso stepped up to him to grab the weapon as it toppled.

They were both reaching for the muzzle-loader, their eyes on the wavering gunstock, and several of the other young men were stepping forward in an effort to help them when the gun exploded with a thunderous roar. Bits of shining metal flew arcing through the air, and before they started dropping to the ground, their glints and all the area around the explosion were blotted out by a cloud of yellowish smoke that spread rapidly in billows that hid the scene from Longarm and Moore.

"Whoever got that muzzle-loader ready must've put in two or three times as much powder as they ought've,"

165

Longarm said without taking his eyes off the scene of the blast.

"It's all I can think of that might've happened," Moore agreed. "Chances are, they either crammed in too much powder when they loaded it, or the barrel had a crack in it that nobody noticed."

"It could've been either one," Longarm agreed. "And I'd say it's not likely that too many in that bunch is going to come outa that blast alive."

Cries of pain were coming from the smoke cloud now, but the dense yellow haze seemed to grow larger rather than to diminish. Then at the edges of the obscured area the dark blots of running figures could be seen. In a moment the runners emerged from the still-spreading but thinning smoke. They scattered as they ran, and Longarm tried to count them, but they were moving too fast and changing directions too rapidly.

As though the blast of the exploding rifle had been a cue, a low moaning like a requiem began sounding from Whistle Rock. Longarm and Moore glanced toward the column in time to see its mushroomlike cap begin to sway. They watched it in fascination as it moved back and forth. Then the jagged-faced column that supported it began to crumble. The sighing whistle faded and died. For a moment the cap-rock seemed to be suspended in midair before it crashed as the center of the column collapsed, and instead of the towering shaft a pile of indiscriminate earth and stone stood in its place.

By this time the powder smoke that hung so thickly over the spot where the muzzle-loader exploded had started thinning to a transparent haze. Sprawled motionless figures of those killed by the rupturing gun's blast lay scattered on the ground.

"I don't like to see men killed that way, not having no chance to fight back at all," Longarm said to Ben Moore. His voice was level, undisturbed, as he went on. "But they wasn't giving us no chance, so I guess it's all evened out."

"I'd say they killed themselves by being careless." Moore frowned. "We're certainly not to blame."

"Let's start getting free," Longarm suggested. He nodded toward the body-littered scene of the explosion as he went on. "Them fellows that run off was too spooked to take our rifles when they begun scooting, and if I ain't seeing things, that's the butt of my Colt sticking up outa that blanket yonder. Soon as we can we got to go over there and get our guns. And I got a real hankering to light me a cigar. I got plenty of 'em, and matches too, in my pocket, but I can't get to 'em."

"Damn it, Longarm!" Moore exclaimed. "How you can think about something like a cigar at a time like this is beyond me! Here we just missed getting killed and you want a smoke!"

"Sure, but I can wait till we've got ourselves free to get away from here," Longarm replied.

"And how to you aim to do that?" Moore asked. "Even if we had knives to cut these leather strips, we couldn't get to them with our wrists tied in back of us like they are."

"There's a way to do most anything, if a man sets his mind to it and don't have no squeamishness about hurting himself a little bit."

As Longarm spoke he was bending his shoulders forward. As he watched Longarm's moves, Moore could see that the strain placed on the leather thongs that held his hands behind his back had caused them to cut cruelly

167

into his wrists, and those that had been passed around his chest were creasing into his rib cage. He glanced at Longarm's face, and was surprised to see that it showed no signs of pain from the cutting pressure of the leather thongs.

Suddenly Longarm relaxed the pressure by pushing the ground with his feet and rearing back against the sapling. His move shook the little tree's trunk. It quivered and its barren branches shivered. Longarm's movements had cut deeply into the sapling's fragile bark, and it had also stretched the rawhide thongs a tiny bit. For a moment, Longarm leaned back against the trunk of the small tree. Then he repeated his earlier maneuver. The tree trunk quivered as it took the strain for a second time, and around the areas where the thongs passed the bark began to fall in splintered shreds.

When Longarm leaned back against the sapling's trunk a third time, small spurts and shreds of bark dropped from the tree's trunk where the thin strips of leather had cut deep creases in it. The scored stripes now revealed bare wood, gleaming whitely in contrast to the dark striated bark, and the bindings around Longarm's chest were no longer taut. They sagged a bit now. Longarm twisted his wrists and worked his hands around in semicircles, and the blacksmith could see that now Longarm could move almost freely.

"One more time oughta do it," Longarm told Moore.

His voice was a bit taut, but Moore could not catch any hint in it of the pain he knew Longarm must be feeling. He watched while Longarm tensed his muscles and pressed against the leather strips in a third effort.

Now, when Longarm relaxed after pressing against the leather strips again, there was an appreciable loosening of the strips that bound him to the tree. He began twisting his body from side to side, bending his knees now and then, and hunching his shoulders forward. When he stood erect this time, Moore could see that the leather bindings were very slack indeed.

Longarm started twisting now. Bit by bit his movements grew freer. At last he managed to pull one hand free from the bindings that encircled his wrists. After opening and closing his hand, flexing his fingers now and then, Longarm set his jaws and yanked his left arm free. The suddenly slacked strips flew apart and Longarm shook himself to speed their fall to the ground.

"Them Indians didn't know how much leather stretches when a man puts all his muscle into pulling against it," Longarm told Moore.

As he spoke, Longarm was taking out his pocketknife. He stepped up to Moore and slashed the leather strips that held him to the tree. Moore moved away from the tree trunk as the bits of leather dropped to the ground. Longarm stepped back, snapping the blade of his knife closed.

"I'll admit I don't know how you managed to do all that," Moore said. "For a while there, I got the idea we'd be lashed tight to those trees till we starved to death and rotted."

"Why, a man can do most anything he tries to, if he presses hard enough," Longarm told the blacksmith. "A course, he's got to keep his wits about him and know when to push and when not to."

As he spoke, Longarm was fumbling a cigar out of his pocket. The thin cylinder was bent and its wrapper loosened. He licked the cigar and straightened it as best he could, then drew his thumbnail across the head of a match and puffed until the tip was glowing steadily.

"Hadn't we better get moving?" Moore asked. "The Sinkiuses are likely to get over being spooked and come back."

"I figure they will," Longarm said. "But by then we'll be well on our way. All we got to do is pick up our rifles and pistol and gather up the rest of our gear. We know our horses are up at that place where they penned us up, and I misdoubt that we'll be pushed for time."

"But they will be back," Moore protested.

"Maybe. Maybe not," Longarm said as they started toward the rifles that still lay undisturbed on the ground where the fleeing Indians had dropped them. "I got a hunch that whistling rock falling down like it did is going to spook 'em away from here worse than anything we might or mightn't do."

"You think it'll take them a while to get over being afraid to come back again?"

"It's likely," Longarm answered. "But that ain't here nor there."

"You've got Sully Briggs in mind now, I suppose?"

"He's the one we started after," Longarm agreed. "Him and that Kelly Sisson. If I had to choose between 'em, I'd go after Sisson first, but my hunch is that him and Briggs ain't too far apart from each other. How much outa the way did we get from where they was heading?"

"Not too much," Moore replied. "We won't have a lot further to go before we get to that land of Sully's, once we're back on the main trail."

"I figure you knowing how the ground lays up here in the Scablands is going to save a pretty good bit of time," Longarm observed. "And you're right as rain about us

170

hurrying up to move on. I'll tell you something else. I won't be stretching the truth one little bit when I say that I don't ever aim to get close to this place here again."

"That little nap we stopped to take sure helped a lot," Longarm told Moore as they swung up into their saddles. "And from what you said you figured when we stopped, we ain't got much further to go."

Moore pointed ahead, where a low ridge of raw earth defied all of nature's laws by stretching across the land in a perfectly straight line.

"That's Sully's way of marking his boundaries," he told Longarm. "Oh, he's not the only one who uses it. Most of the folks who try to settle in here can't spare money for fences, so they just toss up one of those ridges along a boundary line."

"Then his property lays on the other side of it," Longarm noted. "And I reckon his house'll be a little ways further along?"

"Not house," Moore said. "Dugout."

"When we was talking on the trail up, I thought you said you hadn't been here before," Longarm said.

"I haven't. The only reason I know that is because the poor devil Sully squeezed this piece of land out of came to my shop before he left, trying to sell his farming gear. He didn't have much, just a hoe and a rake and a couple of shovels. I bought them off of him, but he told me the price I offered was a whole lot better than Sully's. He told me about his dugout while we were dickering."

"Well, now. That sorta changes what little smidge of plans I been mulling over since we started," Longarm said. His frown was a bit more pronounced now.

"In what way?"

"Why, if we get into any kind of fracas with them rascals, it'd be a whole lot easier to get at 'em in a farm shanty than it would be if they're in a dugout. Dirt stops bullets a sight better than planks."

"You think it's going to come to shooting?" Moore asked.

"If we was after Sully by himself, I'd say no. He'd be more likely to go along peaceful if it comes to arresting him," Longarm said. "He'd figure he could buy his way outa just about any scrape he got into."

"Which I suppose he could," Moore noted. "When you're as rich as Sully is."

"But Kelly Sisson's a different piece of goods. He's thinking about that rope that's waiting for him when I get him back to the pen."

"I can see that he wouldn't have a lot to lose."

"But I reckon it's like my grandma used to tell me when I was a little tad growing up back in West Virginia," Longarm went on. "What can't be cured has to be endured, so come along. Let's get on with the hog-butchering."

Nudging their horses ahead, Longarm and Moore started toward the ridge of earth.

Chapter 14

"Was we to try working a hook the size we'd need to yank Kelly Sisson out of a dugout with, it might turn out to be a mite too heavy for us to handle," Longarm remarked as he and Moore rode across the barren soil toward the hump of excavated earth that marked the entrance to the dugout. Gesturing toward the elongated dirt pile, he went on. "That settler sure must've done a bunch of digging."

"Seeing how much dirt he's got humped up there, I'd have to agree with you," Moore said. "And unless I'm wrong, the bigger the dugout is, the more trouble we'll have pinning down Sully and that escaped prisoner we're after."

"You've learned a lot real fast," Longarm said approvingly. "And so far you've pretty much been right, but sometimes trouble sorta works both ways."

"I guess I've still got some learning to do." Moore

173

frowned. "Just how do you mean that?"

"It's easy one-two-three," Longarm replied. "Now I got a close look at all that dirt he's taken out gives me the idea it might be a pretty good-sized place under there. Maybe it's even got two or three rooms. Now, that might give them a little edge, but it might just as easy favor us. It all depends on what happens, and there ain't any way I've been able to figure out which way things is going to go."

"I suppose you're the one who'd know best about that," Moore said. "But since you mentioned that you've had to get wanted men out of tight places before, I had an idea that you might come up with a trick or two that would make the job easier this time."

"Well, now, there's tricks to every trade," Longarm replied. "And I got to admit, I use 'em. Not all of 'em works all the time, but some of 'em works enough times to make it worth knowing the rest. That ain't to say I know all there is, but I reckon I've learned my share."

"I hope you've got a special trick up your sleeve to use getting this Sisson fellow out of whatever hole Sully Briggs has led him to," Moore said. "Because we're getting closer and closer to that pile of dirt, and I can't help wondering what's going to happen when we reach it."

"Why, that'll most likely depend on what Sully and Kelly Sisson does. Like I've told you, I can't just shoot a man down without giving him a chance to give up peaceful, not even if it's the kind of a killer like Sisson is."

"Or Sully Briggs?"

"Him either," Longarm replied. "But just let your nerves rest easy, Ben. If I ain't worrying about you, there ain't no cause for you to be worrying about yourself."

Longarm and Moore had maintained their slow

174

advance while they talked. Now they were within a few feet of the big earth pile. Near the center it rose above to the level of their horses' heads. The heaped dirt spread over the ground in a rough arc, curving away from them for a dozen yards on each side of its center, the ends dropping in a gentle slant to ground level. In the center of the curve and a bit beyond the point where the base of the huge soil heap began, two shovels were sticking up, their handles crossed, their blades buried in the soil.

Now from the vantage point of their saddles Longarm and Moore could see the rough black arch of the entrance to the dugout, just beyond the earth pile. Longarm reined in, and Moore pulled up his horse. For a moment Longarm paid no attention to his companion, but took out a cigar and flicked a match into flame. He puffed until the end of the stogie glowed red.

"Damned if you're not about the coolest customer I've ever run into," Moore observed. "Sitting here waiting for a killer and a swindler to show up and maybe start shooting, and you just go ahead and light up like you were leaning back in an easy chair in your own parlor!"

"Why, it don't do no good for a man to get his bowels in an uproar," Longarm replied. His voice was level, almost mild. "I found out a long time ago that getting all excited don't help things out a mite, and—"

He broke off suddenly and stood up in his stirrups. Leaning toward Moore, he gave the blacksmith a hearty shove that sent him tumbling out of his saddle. As Longarm kicked his feet free from his stirrups and rolled out of his own saddle to land on the ground a shot cracked from beyond the earth pile. The whine of the bullet whistled over their heads as it sped to a wasted burial somewhere beyond them in the barren Scablands soil.

175

Longarm had landed in a sprawl and Moore had fallen on his back beside his horse. He lay where he'd landed, watching Longarm rising to his knees.

"Just keep your head down and stay right where you are for a minute," Longarm told him. "Don't waste no shells shooting back unless them two bastards inside show themselves, which I don't figure they'll be fool enough to do."

"How'd you know they were going to come out shooting?" Moore asked. "I sure didn't see or hear anything."

"Well, you know the tricks of your trade about like I do mine. I just happened to see a little glint of light that couldn't't've come from nothing but a gun barrel," Longarm explained. "It wasn't nothing but just plain luck that I seen it in time to get us outa the way of that sneak shot one of them fellows in the dugout was figuring he'd try for."

"I'm not going to argue on that," Moore told him. "And I'd say you saw it just in time."

"It saved our bacon," Longarm agreed. "But luck works both ways, Ben. Now, the good luck is we've got this far pretty easy. The bad luck is that they've found out we're here before we could get close enough to bottle 'em up in that dugout and grab 'em."

"What do we do now?" Moore asked.

"That's what I been trying to figure." Longarm's voice relected a new assurance as he went on. "We're in the catbird seat right now, but that ain't saying it'll stay that way. Now, them two in back of that dirt pile know damn well they can't just walk out and give up, so they're apt to be getting a mite twitchy."

"By that, you mean they'll come out shooting."

"Likely they will. And I don't know about Sully

176

Briggs, but that Kelly Sisson's too old of a hand to fall for any of the tricks I got in my book."

"Where does that leave us then?"

"Oh, we still got the edge," Longarm assured him. "We're pretty much able to move around, and they're tied down. We don't have to—" He broke off as he heard his name called from the other side of the massive earthen barrier.

"Long! Marshal Long!" The voice coming from the shelter of the earthen embankment was that of Sully Briggs.

Dropping his own voice to a whisper, Longarm told Moore, "I been wondering when they'd pop up and ask for a little parley. Let's see what they got in mind."

"You don't think they're offering to give up, do you?"

Longarm shook his head as he replied, "They're likely smart enough to know we wouldn't listen to 'em, no matter how much they was to offer. But maybe Sully Briggs just ain't got it through his head yet that all the money he's got ain't enough to let him buy his way outa every scrape he gets into."

"What about Kelly Sisson?"

"He just plain ain't about to let me get my hands on him again. He knows there's a hangman's rope waiting for him when I deliver him back to the pen."

Apparently, Briggs had grown impatient, for now he raised his head above the dirt pile and called, "Marshal Long! Are you going to come talk to me, or ain't you?"

"I just can't quite figure out what we got to talk about," Longarm shouted back. "You ain't got nothing I want, and I sure as hell ain't going to give you what you want."

"Damn it, Long, you haven't even heard my offer yet!"

"Which oughta give you the idea that I ain't interested in listening to it," Longarm called. "But if you been figuring to buy me off, just give it up. I ain't selling my badge to you nor nobody else!"

Longarm had not been devoting all his attention to Briggs. He'd kept his eyes moving from one end of the dirt pile to the other. He caught the glint of sunlight reflected from gunmetal when Sisson raised the muzzle of his rifle. When jailbreaker's head rose above the rim of the dirt embankment to sight his shot, Longarm had his own rifle shouldered and his trigger finger ready.

He glimpsed Sisson's movement and sighted quickly, then squeezed off his shot. A puff of dried earth spurted at the top of the earthen barricade that sheltered Sisson and Briggs. The heads of both men dropped from sight. Longarm was pumping a fresh round into his rifle when Ben Moore's shot echoed in his ears. He got a fleeting glimpse of the two fugitives behind the earthen barricade as they dived into the dugout's doorway, and instead of shouldering his Winchester, he lowered its muzzle.

"Looks like they figured they'd be better off taking cover," he told his companion.

"I saw them too," Moore replied. "But I don't handle a rifle as fast as you."

"I sure wasn't fast enough that time," Longarm said. "But I'd say they just as good as quit when they dived in the door of that dugout." He shook his head. "There ain't no way they'll get away from us now."

"Maybe all that we need to do is go up to the dugout door and tell them to come out," Moore suggested.

"You don't think they'll be softheaded enough to stay in there, do you?"

"Why not?" Moore asked. "There's no other way for

178

them to get out, if that dugout's like all the others I've run into."

"Maybe you got a point at that," Longarm noted. "Let's just keep our eyes peeled while we ride on up there."

Remounting and nudging their horses ahead, Longarm and Moore started them at a walk toward the embankment. As they drew closer to it Longarm signaled with a wave for his companion to slant off to ride to the other end. Moore nodded as he reined his horse in its new path.

Keeping close watch on the tunnel's yawning black mouth, they completed their approach without drawing fresh gunfire from the pair in the dugout. As they started to ride toward each other, Moore raised his eyebrows in a question and Longarm gestured for him to pull up before they reached the door. Dismounting, they walked cautiously with rifles ready until they stood facing one another on opposite sides of the gloomy-looking opening.

After nodding to Moore, Longarm raised his voice and called, "You two in there! Throw your guns out and come out with your arms up!"

Kelly Sisson's coarse voice sounded in reply. "Like hell we will! You'll have to come in after us!"

Moore caught Longarm's attention with a gesture, dropped his voice, and asked as he pointed to the yawning opening, "Are we both going in at the same time?"

"I ain't going to say yes or no," Longarm replied in the same half-whisper. "But if you got a mind to, I'd be right glad to have your company."

When they reached the doorway Longarm took a quick step or two and placed himself in the lead. Moore followed him into the dugout. For a step or two the way was clear. A length of wide cloth stretched across the passageway and hid what lay beyond it. Motioning to Moore to stand with his back pushed against the earthen wall, Longarm extended his Colt to arm's length and pulled the curtain back with the revolver's muzzle.

He'd been waiting for the shot that came from behind the curtain and set the cloth swaying. Pulling back his gun hand, Longarm waited for the motion of the fabric to end. Subdued whispers broke the silence that settled down when the echoes of the shot had faded and died away. Neither Longarm nor Moore could decipher the unintelligible sounds.

Frowning in the transparent gloom, Moore looked questioningly at Longarm and gestured toward the cloth door. Longarm shook his head. He was hugging the dirt wall and he gestured for Moore to do the same. The young blacksmith did not move back a moment too soon. He'd no sooner flattened himself against the wall than a shot roared, its sound like thunder in the narrow passage.

With a sullen thunk the slug hit the wall a few inches from Longarm's shoulder, and before the brief echoes of its impact had died away the shot was followed by others, the barking of Sisson's and Carter's weapons. A silence fell when the echoes ended and Longarm started to raise his hand in a motion to signal that the time had finally come to attack.

He stopped the moving hand before he'd lifted it an inch when a strange creaking and groaning noise began. It seemed to come from everywhere and nowhere. Longarm wasted no time, for he'd heard much the same noise before.

He closed the gap between him and Moore with a long

quick step, grabbed Moore's arm, and started pulling him to the doorway. If the first creaking sound had been a whisper, the next was almost an explosion. By the time it started Longarm had half led, half dragged Moore down the earth-walled corridor and into the welcome freshness of the warm air outside.

More muffled noises were sounding from inside the soddy when they reached the exit and were standing in the welcome sunshine. Both Longarm and Moore still held their weapons.

"How long do you think it'll take those two inside to dig out?" Moore asked.

"They ain't never coming out," Longarm said.

Moore was silent for a moment, then he asked, "You're sure?"

"Certain-sure. If that dirt fall didn't squeeze the life out of 'em, they'd be suffocated by now. I seen a few miners all squashed up by dirt-falls like that one. I used to carry water buckets down into mines like that one when I was a tad back in West Virginia."

"Then all we've got left to do—" Moore began, but got no further when Longarm interrupted him.

"All we got to do is ride back to town," he said. "You'll be getting anxious to get your shop going again."

"Will you be staying around town a while?"

"Not likely," Longarm replied. "I got to go back to my headquarters and write out a lot of reports. It'll take me as long to do that as it's taken me to get this case closed. About all I'll have time to do when we get back to Moses is have a sip of Tom Moore's rye whiskey and—" He stopped as a smile grew on his face. "And maybe say good-bye to some of the folks I met there. That just might keep me around a day or two longer."

181

Watch for

LONGARM AND THE SKULL CANYON GANG

150th novel in the bold
LONGARM series from Jove

Coming in June!

A special offer for people who enjoy reading the best Westerns published today. If you enjoyed this book, subscribe now and get . . .

TWO FREE

A $5.90 VALUE—NO OBLIGATION

If you enjoyed this book and would like to read more of the very best Westerns being published today, you'll want to subscribe to True Value's Western Home Subscription Service. If you enjoyed the book you just read and want more of the most exciting, adventurous, action packed Westerns, subscribe now.

Each month the editors of True Value will select the 6 very best Westerns from America's leading publishers for special readers like you. You'll be able to preview these new titles as soon as they are published, FREE for ten days with no obligation.

TWO FREE BOOKS

When you subscribe, we'll send you your first month's shipment of the newest and best 6 Westerns for you to preview. With your first shipment, two of these books will be yours as our introductory gift to you absolutely FREE, regardless of what you decide to do. If you like them, as much as we think you will, keep all six books but pay for just 4 at the low subscriber rate of just $2.45 each. If you decide to return them, keep 2 of the titles as our gift. No obligation.

Special Subscriber Savings

When you become a True Value subscriber you'll save money several ways. First, all regular monthly selections will be billed at the low subscriber price of just $2.45 each. That's

WESTERNS!

at least a savings of $3.00 each month below the publishers price. Second, there is never any shipping, handling or other hidden charges—Free home delivery. What's more there is no minimum number of books you must buy, you may return any selection for full credit and you can cancel your subscription at any time. A TRUE VALUE!

Mail the coupon below

To start your subscription and receive 2 FREE WESTERNS, fill out the coupon below and mail it today. We'll send your first shipment which includes 2 FREE BOOKS as soon as we receive it.

Mail To:
True Value Home Subscription Services, Inc.   10570
P.O. Box 5235
120 Brighton Road
Clifton, New Jersey 07015-5235

YES! I want to start receiving the very best Westerns being published today. Send me my first shipment of 6 Westerns for me to preview FREE for 10 days. If I decide to keep them, I'll pay for just 4 of the books at the low subscriber price of $2.45 each; a total of $9.80 (a $17.70 value). Then each month I'll receive the 6 newest and best Westerns to preview Free for 10 days. If I'm not satisfied I may return them within 10 days and owe nothing. Otherwise I'll be billed at the special low subscriber rate of $2.45 each; a total of $14.70 (at least a $17.70 value) and save $3.00 off the publishers price. There are never any shipping, handling or other hidden charges. I understand I am under no obligation to purchase any number of books and I can cancel my subscription at any time, no questions asked. In any case the 2 FREE books are mine to keep.

Name _____

Address _____ Apt. # _____

City _____ State _____ Zip _____

Telephone # _____

Signature _____
(if under 18 parent or guardian must sign)
Terms and prices subject to change.
Orders subject to acceptance by True Value Home Subscription Services, Inc.